"I already spoke to your father."

Kathleen cocked her head to one side. "About what?"

As he'd told her, he should just say it. "Courting you. And he gave his permission."

Her sweet expression turned to confusion. "You what? Why would you do that?"

"Don't tell me you didn't expect this?"

With her feet, she pushed the swing back away from Noah until she stood with the seat at her back. "You had no right to ask him." She untangled herself from the ropes.

"But he already gave his permission. What will I tell him?"

"I don't know. Don't you understand? I can't court you."

"Why not? Is there someone else?" The thought of someone else courting her twisted his insides.

"I can't court anyone because I'm never going to get married."

"Never? Why not? You're still young."

"Because God called me to be a doctor. If I marry, I won't be able to be a doctor. It's a sacrifice I made a long time ago."

Mary Davis is an award-winning author of more than a dozen novels. She is a member of American Christian Fiction Writers and is active in two critique groups. Mary lives in the Colorado Rocky Mountains with her husband of thirty years and three cats. She has three adult children and one grandchild. Her hobbies are quilting, porcelain doll making, sewing, crafts, crocheting and knitting. Please visit her website, marydavisbooks.com.

Books by Mary Davis

Love Inspired

Prodigal Daughters
Courting Her Amish Heart

Love Inspired Heartsong Presents

Her Honorable Enemy
Romancing the Schoolteacher
Winning Olivia's Heart

Courting Her Amish Heart

Mary Davis

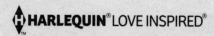
HARLEQUIN® LOVE INSPIRED®

Recycling programs
for this product may
not exist in your area.

LOVE INSPIRED BOOKS

ISBN-13: 978-1-335-42793-9

Courting Her Amish Heart

www.Harlequin.com

Printed in U.S.A.

For do I now persuade men, or God? or
do I seek to please men? for if I yet pleased men,
I should not be the servant of Christ.
—*Galatians* 1:10

Dedicated to my awesome sister Kathleen Shogren.

Aller Anfang ist schwer. "All beginnings are hard."

Chapter One

Kathleen Yoder stood in front of the motel room mirror, fussing with her hair. She had to look just right. She needed to be viewed as a proper Amish woman if her community was going to welcome her home. She pulled the pins from her hair and started over. What did the English say? Third time's a charm.

Even though all through her medical training she had continued to dress Amish and put her hair up, she hadn't had another Amish woman to measure her ability against. It wasn't *gut* to compare oneself to others, but she could gauge if she had been getting her clothes and hair put right. Iron sharpens iron. Had the fourteen years in the English world whittled away at her Amish standards? Probably. However, she would quickly fall back into Amish life.

She snugged her *kapp* on her head and

smoothed her hands down her blue Plain dress. At this point, no more amount of labor would make her appearance any more appropriate. She would need to trust *Gott* to pave her way.

She zipped her suitcase closed, lowered it to the floor and extended the roller handle, holding it tight. With her other hand, she slung one strap of her backpack of medical supplies over her shoulder and draped her coat over her arm.

Rolling her suitcase behind her, she opened the door and stepped out into the sunlight. The only things that stood between her and home now were the bus ride to Goshen and the walk to the farm. If she could convince the bus driver to let her off outside of town, she would have only eight miles to trek.

She traipsed to the bus station three blocks away, purchased her ticket and sat in the seat behind the driver. "Could you let me off outside of Goshen?" She gave him the country road names of the intersection.

"Sorry. I'm not authorized to make a stop there." He tipped his head up and glanced at her in his rearview mirror. "Is someone meeting you at the station?"

"No." She hadn't had the courage to contact anyone to come get her. It would be harder to turn her away if she were at the door.

"How you getting from town out to the country?"

"I'll walk."

"That's a long ways. Well over ten miles."

Thirteen point two from the city limits and another two or three from the bus station. "I'll be fine." She needed to get used to traversing these stretches. No time like the present.

"I'm sure one of your people would gladly come into town to get you. Or you could take a taxi."

If someone knew she was returning today. But she hadn't told anyone. "The walk will do me *gut*." It would help transition her back into the slower pace of life. As well as giving her something to occupy herself with instead of dealing with idle chatter. Giving her a chance to prepare herself for the meeting of *her people*. She hoped they still *were* her people.

She stared out the window at her home state's terrain sweeping by. As the Indiana countryside grew increasingly more familiar, snippets of her past surged through her. Places she'd been. People she'd seen. Homes she'd visited. Her life among the English fell away with each passing mile.

The bus slowed, and the driver pulled onto the shoulder of the highway and stopped under an overpass. The one she'd hoped he could have taken to shorten her walk. The driver stood and faced the passengers. "I need to check something on the bus outside. Won't be but a minute." The driver gazed directly at Kathleen. "Could you accompany me?"

Kathleen stood. "All right." She didn't know what help she could be.

With a broad smile, he motioned for her to precede him down the steps.

Once outside, he handed over her medical pack and coat. He must have taken them from her seat. He pointed to the lower storage compartments. "Which one's your luggage in?"

"Excuse me?"

He faced her. "You see, I'm not supposed to stop along the way, but if I think there could be a problem with the bus…well, that's a different story. And if, while I'm checking the bus, a passenger was to get off, and if I wasn't able to talk her into getting back on, there's nothing I could do about that. And if a particular piece of luggage were to 'fall' off, there wouldn't be anything I could do about that either. Seeing as I wouldn't notice it until I got to the station."

She smiled. "I appreciate your kindness."

"I don't know what you're talking about. I'm just checking on the bus." He winked. "I believe the problem could be in the back compartment. I'll need to move a…dark blue roller case?"

She nodded. She shouldn't encourage this kind of deceptive behavior.

He opened the section and pushed a couple of bags aside before pulling hers free. "You going to be all right by yourself?"

"I'll be fine." She felt safer already being here than she'd ever felt being at the university or in any of the hospitals or clinics where she'd worked. "Thank you." She appreciated him cutting her walk in half.

Giving her a nod, he climbed back into the bus. "False alarm. Everything is as it should be." He winked at her again, then closed the doors.

She waved in return, and several passengers waved to her. As the bus pulled away, she pressed a hand to her queasy abdomen. Almost home. Regardless of the reception she would receive, she was back in her Elkhart County New Order Amish community. She draped her coat over the top of her suitcase, balanced her medical backpack on top of that, gripped the roller handle and struck out on the very last leg of her fourteen-year journey. Up the off-ramp, down the road, along the country lane, and toward home.

After trudging along for fifteen minutes or so on the edge of the blacktop, she realized this was not at all like walking the halls of a hospital. She was out of shape and shifted her suitcase handle to her other hand.

The familiar reverberation of horse's hooves

clomping on the pavement came from behind her. The comforting sound both thrilled her and caused her unsteady insides to knot. In all her daydreams, she hadn't pictured seeing any Amish until her family opened the front door. How foolish. Who would this be? Someone she knew? Would anyone still recognize her?

As the horse and buggy drew closer, her midsection twisted tighter and tighter. She dared not turn around though she wanted to know whom it was. But at the same time, she didn't want to know. Let them pass her by.

First, the horse came alongside her, then the buggy. The driver slowed the horse to her pace. *"Hallo."*

She glanced up into the sun and raised her hand to shade her eyes. The bearded face held a kind smile and sparkling brown eyes that sent a small thrill dancing through her. Shame on her. His beard signified he was a married man. Though he seemed familiar, she couldn't place him. Maybe it was just because he was Amish. And all her emotions, negative and positive, were heightened.

"Hallo." She stopped, welcoming the respite. Or did she welcome the delay in arriving at her destination?

He reined in the horse and spoke in *Deutsch.* "Can I give you a ride?"

It had been so long since she'd heard her language. She replied in kind. "That's very considerate of you." She was tired, not used to this amount of walking in the late-spring heat. "But I'm fine. Walking is *gut*." Nevertheless, she remained rooted in place, not wanting to part company from this man yet for some strange reason.

He set the brake and jumped down. He stood between her and a passing pickup truck as though protecting her from it. His gaze flickered to her suitcase then back to her face. "I'm Noah Lambright."

No doubt he thought she was running away with her suitcase in tow. "I'm Kathleen Yoder."

His eyes widened slightly as though her name were familiar. Why wasn't his? *Noah?* She had known many Noahs in her youth, both young and old. But now she'd spent nearly as much time away as she had at home. Certainly such a handsome Amish man she would have remembered. "I'm sure my strolling alongside the road with my suitcase must have you confused. I'm not running away, if that's what you're thinking." Quite the opposite. She was finally running home. Home to her family. Home to her community. Home to her Amish way of life. And for some reason, it was important that this man—this Noah—knew that.

"If you were running away, you'd be heading in that direction." He pointed down the road the way she'd come. He picked up her medical pack and coat in one hand and hoisted her suitcase in the other.

Kathleen reached for them. "What are you doing with my things?"

He put them in the back of his open buggy. "Even if you refuse a ride, I can at least take your belongings to your destination so you don't have to cart them along behind you." He held out his hand to her. "Are you sure you don't want a ride? This is the hottest part of the day."

"What would your wife say to you picking up a woman you don't know?"

Pain flickered across his features and left just as quickly. "I'm widowed."

"Oh. I'm so sorry."

"Don't worry about it. She passed three years ago."

"I thought with your beard…" She needed to just stop talking. But why did he still wear one? It wasn't her place to ask. So he *wasn't* married after all. That was *gut* to know. *Ne*, it wasn't. The poor man had lost his wife. And she had no room in her life to consider courting and marriage.

He must have noticed her staring because he

rubbed his jaw. "I've been meaning to shave this off. Thought about doing so this morning."

Three years? And he still wore a beard? That was none of her business.

"So what do you say to that ride?" His mouth quirked up on one side.

That caused her insides to dance. Though she didn't want to hurry her journey along, she certainly wasn't enjoying the hike. She *had* wanted this time alone to gather her thoughts. But her hand reached out for his.

Strong, calloused and work worn. Comforting.

He helped her up into the front seat and with him came the distinct aroma of fresh-cut wood and something sweet.

She had rarely ever ridden in the front. This was an open buggy and still daylight, so there wouldn't be anything inappropriate about accepting his offer. For what she had spent the past fourteen years doing and what she planned to do in the near future, she needed to make sure everything else she did was beyond reproof. She didn't want to give the church leadership any more reasons than necessary to refuse her offer of help.

He climbed in next to her and set the buggy into motion. Strangely, he didn't dive into conversation and questions like the English, who felt the need to fill every silence. He just drove. Down one road and then another. Turning here and there. How odd that the silence wasn't in the least awkward. Sitting next to this man—this stranger—was comfortable.

And honey. He smelled of wood and *honey*. Very comforting, indeed.

Solar panels winking off a roof caught her attention. An *Englisher* must have bought that farm. When she'd left, it had belonged to one of the Lehman families. Another house also had solar panels. And then the next one. They couldn't have all been sold out of the community. Amish liked to keep Amish property in the family, and if not, sell it to another Amish. "Did *Englishers* buy several of these farms?"

"Ne."

"But what about the solar panels? They aren't allowed."

"They are now."

She'd thought about how nice this form of electricity would be for the Amish and planned to bring it up to the leaders—after she got her clinic going. What other changes had taken place in her absence? Did her parents have solar panels?

When he turned onto the road that passed her

parents' home, she faced him. "How did you know where I was going?"

"You're Kathleen Yoder. Your parents are David and Pamela Yoder."

"How did you know?"

"Everyone knows who you are. The girl who went away to become a doctor."

She couldn't tell if that was sarcasm in his voice or something…something less negative. Dare she hope admiration? What was she thinking? Of course not. Her devout Amish neighbors would never condone her actions without permission from the bishop. But that didn't matter. She would help them whether they liked it or not. She had a plan. In time, she hoped they would see the *gut* in what she'd done.

Lord, let them see I did it for them. For all of them.

Noah clucked to the horse and flicked the reins to keep Fred moving. He still couldn't reconcile the strange sight that he'd found on the roadside.

Kathleen Yoder. Strolling along like a distant memory or faded dream.

She wasn't at all what he'd pictured. He'd heard so many stories about her that he'd thought she'd be taller. More of a person to be reckoned with. He'd expected her to be more forceful. Not demure. How was she ever going to forge her way to be a doctor in their community? A doctor close at hand could prevent many senseless deaths. He admired her tenacity to do what no other Amish would. Woman or man.

And if she could come back after nearly a decade and a half, that gave him hope that another might too.

He certainly never anticipated her to be pretty, with her dark brown hair, steady blue eyes and heart-shaped face. Why would she have wanted to leave and pursue something like medicine against the leadership's wishes? She could have married any man she wanted. Every young man must have had his sights on courting her.

"Stop the buggy." Her words came out half-strangled.

"Why? We're almost there."

"That's why. Please stop. Please." She grabbed the reins and pulled back. Her hands brushed against his.

Fred eagerly obeyed.

Her touch sent a tingle shuddering up Noah's arm. Before he could put on the brake and even before the horse came to a complete stop, Kathleen jumped to the ground and circled behind the buggy.

He set the brake and climbed down.

Kathleen paced behind the buggy, muttering to herself in English. "I stood up to Dr. Wilson with all his old-fashioned treatments that weren't evidence-based. I had been right, and the patient lived. I can do this. I can face my family and the community without shame for my disobedience."

He watched her for a moment. "What are you doing?"

"I'm trying to gain my courage. I thought I'd have this whole walk—" she swung one arm back the way she'd come "—to think about what to say to my parents. Planned it all out. And prepared myself if they don't give me a warm welcome."

"I'm sure they'll welc—"

"What will I say to my younger siblings? Are any of them even left at home? The baby that was born the year after I left. Samuel. He'd be thirteen. And Jessica would be only fifteen. They won't even know me. Are Benjamin and Joshua still enjoying *Rumspringa*? Or are they too old? Have they joined church? And Ruby should be considering marriage. I wonder if she's being courted by anyone? And Gloria is certainly married."

She was really worked up. He felt bad that she

was so distraught. Dare he try again to console her, to let her know all would be well?

Another buggy came up the lane. Noah motioned for the driver to keep going. He didn't think Kathleen needed someone else to witness her distress.

The young man nodded and kept moving.

Noah nodded back.

"Who was that? Someone I would know? Do you think he recognized me?"

"I think you know him. That was Benjamin Yoder."

Kathleen stopped fidgeting and stared at him. "My brother? Benjamin?"

Her steady blue gaze warmed him. He nodded.

With a wistful expression, Kathleen studied the retreating buggy. "My brother." She sighed. "I wouldn't have recognized him. Do you think he recognized me?"

"I don't think he got a very *gut* loo—"

"Of course he didn't recognize me." Kathleen resumed her pacing. "I've been gone for fourteen years, and he was so young when I left. How could he?"

"Kathleen?"

"How will any of them remember me?"

"Kathleen?"

"I will be as a stranger to them. All of them."

Noah grabbed both of her hands to calm her. "Kathleen, look at me."

Her panicked blue eyes turned to him and slowly focused. "I could diagnose pneumonia. I could set a broken bone. I could take out your appendix. All that, I can do. This I cannot." She meant facing her family.

He squeezed her hands. "Don't be silly."

"I'm not silly." She tried to pull her hands free.

He held fast. He didn't want to let her go. "I didn't say *you* were silly. I said you were *being* silly. You left the community and went against the wishes of the church leaders. You studied for so many years. You have done what no other Amish have dared. Where is that girl? The one who did all those things?"

Her voice came out small. "I think I left her back in the city."

"*Ne.* You didn't. *She* brought you back here." He'd presumed she would be a stout woman who took charge. Not this slip of a thing who appeared scared and unsure of herself. Not this beautiful woman standing before him. "Your parents will be happy to see you."

"How do you know?"

"They've never stopped talking about you."

"You know my parents?"

He gave a nod. "I've spent quite a bit of time

with them the past three years. My farm borders theirs. They're proud of all you've accomplished."

"Now I know they've never said that. Pride goes against the church."

"It's the *way* they talk about you."

"So they talk about my being a doctor? Do they think the community will accept me?"

"They don't talk about that."

"You mean my being a doctor?"

He nodded.

"Then how do you know they're proud of my accomplishments, if they don't talk about my being a doctor?"

"Like I said, it's the *way* they talk about you. About their daughter who is in the English world. I can't explain it."

Kathleen pulled free and resumed pacing. "Why did I ever leave? What was I thinking?"

Noah stared at his empty hands, then tucked them into his pockets to keep them from reaching out for her again. "Honestly, I've never been able to figure that out. Did you think the leaders would pat you on the back for your efforts? You know *they* disapprove of your actions? But your *parents* don't."

She stopped and stared at him with wide blue eyes. "I don't know what to do. In a hospital or surgery I do, but not here. Give me a patient, and I'd know what to do."

How could someone be so confident in one area and not in another? "Climb back in the buggy and go see your family. Both you and they have been waiting fourteen years for this. Your reception isn't going to change five minutes from now. Or five hours. Or five days."

"You're right. *Gut* or bad, I must go." She clasped her hands together and bowed her head.

He prayed silently as well. Prayed for a warm welcome. Prayed for Kathleen to be strong. Prayed for Kathleen to become the woman *Gott* meant her to be. Prayed to get to know her better.

After another pickup truck passed, Kathleen marched around the buggy, climbed in and stared straight ahead with her hands folded primly in her lap.

Definitely not how he'd pictured the indomitable Kathleen Yoder. This Kathleen Yoder was never going to make it as a doctor in their Amish district. She would fall back into the traditional Amish role for women or leave the community for *gut* this time. That thought settled uneasily inside him.

Either way, it would be a loss, and he would be disappointed. The community could use her skills and knowledge as a doctor—even if they weren't willing to admit it.

Yet.

No, she wasn't the woman he'd imagined her to be. Hoped her to be.

She was so much better in so many ways.

Chapter Two

Kathleen shifted on the buggy seat as Noah settled next to her. When he flicked the reins and the horse stepped forward, her stomach lurched in tandem with the buggy.

What was wrong with her? She had countered doctors senior to her when a patient was at risk, even grouchy Dr. Wilson. She had taught an undergraduate class. She had stood shoulder to shoulder with other doctors in an operating room.

Or was it this handsome Amish man sitting next to her? Couldn't be. It had to be returning home.

This was her family. Who loved her. And that was the problem. It was one thing to have an arrogant doctor think ill of her, but quite different to have her family view her poorly. That would hurt too much.

Kathleen sat up a little straighter. Regardless of her family's reaction, *Gott* had called her to this path. She had done nothing wrong in His eyes. And wasn't He the one who mattered most?

Noah turned off the road and into her driveway. "Everything will be well. You'll see."

She hoped so. And strangely his words comforted her.

Like the other homes, solar panels sat on the roof.

A tricolor Australian shepherd loped from the barn, barking, announcing their arrival. A dozen or so chickens squawked and scattered.

Noah pulled to a stop and set the brake. When he got out, the dog pranced and leapt around him. "Sit."

The dog raced a few feet away and tore back just as fast.

Making his voice more ominous, he repeated his command. "Sit!" When the dog finally obeyed, it settled at Noah's feet, still wiggling as though it might burst. Noah tousled the shepherd around the neck. "What are you doing here? You should be at home guarding my sheep."

Kathleen stepped down. "This is your dog?"

"*Ja.* She's still young. My other two are supposed to be keeping an eye on her and training her. She does well while I'm on the farm but strays when I'm not there."

She bent toward the dog. "What's her name?"

"Kaleidoscope, on account of her eye."

She looked at the dog's eyes more closely. One brown and the other a patchwork of blues. "Are all your dogs this same breed?"

"I have a black Belgian sheepdog and a black-and-tan Cardigan Welsh corgi."

The Australian shepherd rolled onto her back.

Kathleen obliged by rubbing her tummy. "How old is she?"

"Almost eleven months. She has a lot of growing up to do."

"Noah!" a man called from the barn.

Kathleen froze. Was that her *dat*'s voice? She remained crouched with the dog and stole a glance out of the corner of her eye. The man walking toward them was too young to be her *dat*. Benjamin? He'd grown into a man.

The screen door of the house creaked, and her *mutter* spoke. "Noah, so glad you have come. Who have you brought?"

Air lodged in Kathleen's lungs. She could breathe neither in nor out.

Kaleidoscope flipped from her back to her feet and ran for Benjamin. Fool dog. She was Kathleen's excuse for not looking directly at anyone.

"Someone you're eager to see," Noah said in

a light tone. His deep voice brushed over her, calming some of her nerves.

Still looking at the ground, Kathleen saw three pairs of smallish women's shoes come into view. Her *mum* and sisters?

The time had come. Taking a deep breath, Kathleen stood and gazed directly into her *mum*'s face.

Her *mum*'s smile dropped, and her mouth slipped open. "Kathleen? *My* Kathleen?"

Kathleen nodded. *"Ja, Mum."*

Mum cupped her face in both hands. "You're home." Her eyes glistened.

"I'm home." Kathleen's eyes filled with tears as well.

"I cannot believe this." *Mum* pulled her into her arms. "Finally, my child has returned."

After a moment, Ruby's arms wrapped around her and *Mum*.

"Is that my girl?" Her *dat*'s voice came from beside her.

Both women released her, and her *mum* spoke. "Noah has brought our Kathleen home."

Strangely, she liked the sound of that. *Noah* had brought her.

Beside *Dat* stood Benjamin, who had grown into a strapping young man, as well as Joshua and a gangly Samuel.

Dat gave her a pat on the shoulder in greeting. Exuberant for him. "You know Benjamin and Joshua, but you've not met Samuel."

How old were they all now? She counted in her head. Benjamin would be twenty, Joshua eighteen, and Samuel thirteen. She'd missed so much.

Her brothers each gave a nod.

"Pleased to meet you, Samuel."

He gave her another nod.

Mum hooked her arm around Kathleen. "You remember Ruby."

Her twenty-one-year-old sister smiled. "Of course she does. It's Jessica she might have forgotten. She was only one when you left."

Fifteen-year-old Jessica was the spitting image of *Mum*.

Kathleen took one of Jessica's hands and held it in both of hers. "Naturally I remember you. I carried you around wherever I went."

Mum gave half a laugh. "She was quite put out when you left. No one could console her." Her words weren't said as an admonishment but in loving kindness.

Jessica gave Kathleen a quick hug. "Welcome home."

"Supper will be ready in an hour," *Mum* said. "Noah, you'll stay and eat with us."

Not a question but a command.

He chuckled. "I'd love to."

His laugh warmed Kathleen.

Mum shooed the men away. "Get your work finished so you won't keep supper waiting."

The men—including Noah, leading his horse and buggy—tromped off toward the barn.

Noah glanced over his shoulder as he walked away, and a smile jumped to Kathleen's mouth.

Ruby grasped the handle of the suitcase.

Kathleen reached for it. "I can get that."

"Nonsense. You've had a long trip." Ruby struck out across the yard toward the house.

Mum snatched Kathleen's backpack of medical supplies off the bumping suitcase. And when her coat slid to the ground, Jessica retrieved that. With nothing left for Kathleen to carry, she followed in their wake.

She basked in her family's love. All her trials, doubts and time away would be worth the heartache she'd endured to finally be able to help her people.

Jessica and Samuel might be strangers to her, and she to them, but she looked forward to getting to know them.

Standing shoulder to shoulder with her *mutter* and sisters in the kitchen was both familiar and foreign to Kathleen. The other three obviously had their regular tasks and worked in harmony. Kathleen was more of a hindrance than a help until *Mum* sat her at the table to snap the green beans. In time, she would ease back into the flow of the goings-on in and around the house. Hopefully, that wouldn't take too long.

Noah washed up at the outside spigot with the Yoder men. He had always been welcomed at their table. Even more so since losing Rachel three years ago.

He followed the others inside and sat across the table from Kathleen. Though the shortest of the Yoder women, Kathleen was similar in height to the rest. All between about five-two and five-five. Why had he ever imagined her to be so much taller? And assumed she wouldn't be so pretty?

Seeing Kathleen sitting in the usually empty place always set for her seemed strange. She was finally here to fill the void she'd left. He'd never known this table with her physically here. Her presence had always been felt, even when she wasn't mentioned, by the fact of the vacant chair and unused place setting.

After David said grace, each person filled their plates. Everyone chattered easily except Kathleen. She quietly ate while appearing to enjoy the conversations around her. He tried to listen as she did, a person who had been away for nearly a decade and a half.

Partway through the meal, Samuel asked, "Do we have to call you Doctor now?"

The room became silent. This was what Kathleen had likely feared. Noah wanted to speak up to save Kathleen from having to answer. But why? She was more or less a stranger to him. There was something about her that drew him in. Made him want to protect her.

But her *vater* spoke up. "We'll discuss that another time."

Smoothly avoided, but obviously a tender subject.

Kathleen set her fork down. "I don't mind answering. You are my family. I'm still Kathleen."

Samuel turned back to his plate. One by one, everyone else did the same. Except Kathleen. She looked at each person around the table, then settled her gaze on Noah. He couldn't read her expression, but it flickered between hope and discouragement. He could almost read her thoughts. If her family couldn't accept her being a doctor, how would the rest of the community?

Kathleen averted her gaze first, picking up her fork again and stacking several green beans on it. Nothing but the soft clinking of silverware on plates, swallowing of milk and breathing. The silence in the room resounded as loud as hail pelting the roof.

How much opposition could she take before

she gave up? Though not overt opposition, it was opposition nonetheless. How could such a small slip of a woman stand against the whole community? They would wear her down even though what she was offering could help the community greatly. He ached to help her. But what could he say? It wasn't his place. But still he longed to.

After a couple of minutes of the painful silence, and Kathleen shifting in her seat, she spoke up. "How's the garden faring this year?"

Pamela's shoulders relaxed. "It's doing very well. We've planted several new fruit trees since you—in the past few years."

So that was how it was going to be. Would everyone in the community pretend Kathleen had never left? Pretend she hadn't gone to college? Pretend she wasn't a licensed doctor?

He sighed. Too bad Kathleen had caved under the pressure of silence. What would she do if the leadership decided to shun her for her actions? She would give up for sure. But the table conversation relaxed back into typical Amish discussions about farms and gardens, horses and canning, and barn raisings and quilting. She had put order back into the meal.

Later at home, Noah stared into the mirror. He should have shaved off his beard years ago, but since he never planned to marry again, he didn't see the need. The Lord had been niggling him for months to do it, but he'd ignored the prodding.

The image of Kathleen sprang to his mind. She'd mistakenly thought he had a wife.

It was time. He opened the mirror cabinet over the sink and retrieved scissors, a disposable razor and shaving cream. He pinched his two-inch brown chin whiskers between his thumb and index finger and poised the scissors to snip.

Several breaths passed.

Releasing his beard, he lowered the shears. Was he ready to completely let go of Rachel and their child?

Lord, I know I need to let them go. I should be ready, but I'm not. Please heal my heart.

How many times had he asked that of *Gott*? Enough times to fill his barn.

He leaned his hands on the cold porcelain of the sink and stared at his reflection in the mirror. What was wrong with him that he was still hurting after all this time? *Gott* should be all sufficient for him, so why this empty place still inside? He'd given over his anguish and disappointment each day many, many times, yet every morning they were back like old friends to keep him company.

Too bad Kathleen didn't have something in her medicine bag to fix his heart. What ailed him couldn't be remedied by human efforts. Only by *Gott*.

But somehow, Kathleen's return had helped. Strange.

It was time. Raising the shears once again, he snipped one clump of whiskers after another.

After helping to clean up the kitchen, Kathleen sat with her family in the living room for the evening devotional. The hymns rattled around in her brain. She stumbled over the once-familiar words. They would come back to her.

She had missed this time of day to connect with her family. The last fourteen years of evenings had been spent either poring over medical texts, working in a hospital, or sleeping after coming off a double or triple shift. Exhaustion had been her constant companion. The slower pace of life would be a welcome change as well as the routine of a regular schedule, knowing what to expect from one day to the next.

After the Bible reading, discussion and closing prayer, *Dat* said, "Time for bed."

Her younger siblings all stood, as did Kathleen. "Where will I be sleeping?"

Ruby put her arm around Kathleen's shoulder. "Your bed's still in our room."

Mum tucked her sewing into her basket. "Benjamin took your things up earlier."

Kathleen patted her sister's hand. "I'll be up in a few minutes."

Her brothers and sisters tromped up the stairs, and Kathleen sat back down. She wanted to remain standing but didn't want her parents to feel as though she were lording over them.

Dat leaned forward with a warm expression. "We can't tell you how pleased we are to have you back. We prayed for you every day while you were gone."

"I felt them. Knowing you were praying helped me make it through."

Mum leaned forward. "We wanted to write more."

"I know." Kathleen had received letters the first year or so, then came the letter that said it would be the last. The bishop had requested that they not write her anymore because it would encourage her wayward behavior. Though she hadn't understood the bishop's reasoning, the letter hadn't been a surprise. He would be the toughest of all to convince of the worthiness of her plan.

Dat continued. "We always respected that you needed to make your own decisions."

The point of *Rumspringa*. But she had taken it to an extreme by staying away for fourteen years, just short of half her life, though it felt like more. She wished it hadn't had to be so long, but it had been a necessity to earn her medical degree.

"We appreciate you telling Samuel to call you Kathleen. We must ask you not to refer to yourself as Doctor around the younger ones. They might get the idea we condone your actions and wish it for them as well."

She knew that was a concern and made what she was about to ask all that much harder for them to agree to.

Mum spoke up. "We're proud of you and don't want to tell you what to do. You must make your own choices, but we don't want the others encouraged to do the same. You were always strong-minded and strong in your faith. I always believed that you would return home."

Her *dat* cautioned her further about the church leadership being displeased with her actions. Was Noah disapproving of her actions as well? She hoped not.

She took a deep breath. "I have a request to make." Her parents waited for her to continue, and she did. "I need a place to set up my clinic."

Both her parents leaned back stiffly in their seats.

She hurried on before they could turn her down before hearing her plan. "I want permission to build a small clinic in the side yard. You won't have to do anything. I'll get all the materials and organize the building of it."

After her parents stared at each other for a moment, her *dat* spoke. "What about the church leaders?"

She'd hoped to start building before they realized what she was up to, but she could see that wouldn't be possible. "I'll speak to them after the next community Sunday service. But until then, there wouldn't be anything wrong with putting up a small building on the property. I would like to start staking it out tomorrow."

After a moment of silence, *Dat* said, "I suppose it would be all right to stake it out, but nothing more until you get approval."

He'd said *until* and not *if.* He must believe she would get it. *"Danki."*

"And community church is in three days."

Three days? Kathleen had hoped she was returning with more than a week to polish her planned speech to the leaders. But she supposed that was for the best. No point in putting it off. The sooner she got started the sooner she could start helping people. She went up to bed.

Ruby and Jessica, though in bed, were sitting up, waiting for her. She removed her *kapp* and readied herself for bed.

"Tell us all about living in the English world. What was it like going to university?"

"It was very lonely. People go about doing all manner of things and don't have time for others. They stare at their phones all the time, even when they're talking to you. They bustle around at a frenzied rate. I could hardly catch my breath." *Dat* and *Mum* couldn't have issues with that. Nor the bishop. She had told the truth. "Every day I wanted to be back here with all of you." She flipped the switch on the wall to turn off the light and climbed into bed.

She smiled to herself. How could something like electric lights and electricity make her feel spoiled? After living in the English world for so long, there were some conveniences she didn't want to give up.

She should thank whoever decided solar panels would be a *gut* thing in her Amish community. So many communities didn't allow electricity in any form. Electricity wouldn't distract people from being close to *Gott* but help their lives be easier so they could focus more on Him.

Her eyes popped open in the dark. Those weren't Amish thoughts. *Watch out, Kathleen, or you'll appear too English.* Then Noah *would* disapprove.

Chapter Three

Kathleen woke at five with the image of Noah Lambright at the forefront of her mind. She had been unable to sleep any longer, her nerves on edge. Because she hadn't been around her people for so long, had she grown slack in using careless words? Would she say something inappropriate for her Amish brethren? Would she say something to Noah—or someone else—beyond repair? There seemed to be so many ways she could slip up. *Lord, guard my lips so I don't say anything that will make another stumble in their faith.*

She climbed out of bed, dressed quietly in a green dress and tiptoed downstairs. In the first-floor bathroom, she wrangled her hair and pinned it to the back of her head then pulled on her white *kapp*. She would ask *Mum* if she was putting her hair up right.

Coffee. She required coffee. She put water and grounds in the machine and turned it on. How she'd come to depend on caffeine. Most days, she literally lived on it. She should wean herself down to one or two cups in the morning. For today, she needed to get started right away to rid herself of the caffeine headache already edging its way in. She thanked the Lord again for electricity.

Her first order of business would be to stake out her clinic in the side yard.

As the coffee maker finished filling, *Dat* entered the kitchen. "I thought I heard someone up. I knew it wasn't your *mum*. She'll be down in a minute."

She held up a cup and the carafe. "Want some?"

"Of course."

Kathleen filled the mug and handed it to him. She filled a second cup and set it on the table for *Mum*. Then poured one for herself and added two teaspoons of sugar. Too hot to drink. She breathed in the aroma and could feel the caffeine taking effect already. Was Noah drinking coffee at this moment as well? She dared a small sip of the hot brew. "*Dat*, do you have stakes and string I could use to plan my clinic?"

"In the barn. I'll put them on the front porch

along with a hammer after I finish my before-breakfast chores."

A thrill went through her. He hadn't said *ne*. *"Danki."*

Mum came into the kitchen. "I thought I smelled coffee."

Kathleen pointed to the cup on the table. "That one's cooling for you."

"Danki, dear." She brought it to her face and inhaled deeply, much as Kathleen had done. Some family ties stayed with a person regardless of time and distance.

Dat swigged down the rest of his coffee. "I'll go milk. Be back soon." He walked out.

She turned to *Mum*. "How does he do that without scalding himself?"

Mum chuckled. "I think he turned his mouth and throat to leather so many years ago, he can't feel hot or cold anymore. It's a wonder he can taste anything at all." Her mouth exploded into a smile. "I can't believe you're finally home." With her cup still in hand, she stepped forward and hugged Kathleen.

"I can't believe it either."

Mum released her and wiped her own eyes with her fingertips. "I didn't expect you to be up already. I thought maybe you'd sleep in."

Sleep had eluded her most of the night. It had been a long time since a full eight hours was available for her to sleep. Her body wasn't used to it. It would take time, but she would adjust. "I'm not used to staying in bed for more than three or four hours at a time."

"That's awful. How can you function with so little sleep?"

Kathleen raised her cup aloft. "A lot of caffeine."

"Fresh air and hard work will correct that."

Kathleen nodded. But this work would be easy compared to sixteen-and twenty-four-hour shifts on her feet with only the occasional power nap.

"*Mum*, could you show me how to put my hair up right? I'm afraid I've lost my touch, being away so long." Many days, she'd used a plastic claw clip or had her hair looped through a scrunchie under her *kapp*. Things real Amish women would never do, but she'd usually been too pressed for time. Necessity forced her to find shortcuts. But her hair had always been up and covered. She would not be able to take such measures now.

"Of course. But it'll need to wait until after breakfast."

"I don't want Ruby or Jessica to know."

Mum nodded. "With your *kapp* on, it's fine for now."

"*Danki.*"

After breakfast, *Dat* and the boys left to do their work, and *Mum* sent Ruby and Jessica out to the garden. *Mum* grabbed a chair from the table and guided Kathleen to the bathroom. Kathleen sat, facing the mirror.

Mum removed Kathleen's *kapp* and studied her hair. "You've done pretty well. I'll show you how to make it neater." She pulled the hairpins out. Then, with a spray bottle of water and expert fingers, she twisted the front hair to keep the short hairs under control and wound the rest on the back of Kathleen's head.

Kathleen studied each of *Mum*'s actions so she could get it right on her own tomorrow. Whoever heard of a grown woman needing her *mutter* to put up her hair?

Mum replaced Kathleen's *kapp* and patted her shoulders while gazing at her in the mirror. "There you go."

"Do I look like a proper Amish woman now?" Would Noah approve? Why had she thought of him?

Mum smiled. "Very proper. One more thing—and you're going to like this—buttons!" She pointed to the buttons down the back of her own dress. "A couple of years after you left, they were approved as part of the *Ordnung*."

Kathleen had noticed them but hesitated to say anything. She feared it was one of those things that wasn't quite approved but people did it anyway and others overlooked the infraction. The numerous pins holding her own dress in place poked her sometimes. The one on her left side at her waist was particularly bothersome this morning. She mustn't have gotten it tucked in just right.

"Only white or black buttons. And they must be plain and five-eighths of an inch—no bigger, no smaller."

A long-overdue change. A few women had even started using them before Kathleen left. She didn't understand why such a specific size. Would half of an inch or three-quarters of an inch be a sin?

She chided herself. There went those stray *Englisher* thoughts again. The wrong size buttons would be a sin only because as a church member, one promised to abide by the *Ordnung*. To go against that promise would be disobedience. And disobedience was sin. She needed to get her thinking straight if she was ever going to have a chance at convincing the leadership to allow her to practice medicine in their community. And then there was Noah. For some reason, his opinion of her mattered almost as much as her family's. Strange.

Think like the Amish. Think like the Amish.

Kathleen pushed thoughts of their handsome neighbor aside.

Mum grabbed a produce basket from beside the door. "Let's go help Ruby and Jessica."

"I was going to stake out my clinic. *Dat*'s put what I need on the porch."

Mum tilted her head. "Can't that wait? Your sisters will want to spend time with you. Get to know you."

Kathleen wanted to get reacquainted with her sisters as well. How much could she really accomplish before she got approval? Not much. Now she was glad church was only a few days off and headed out to the garden with *Mum*. Young plants rose healthily from the dirt.

Ruby worked the row to one side of Kathleen. "Tell me about going to university."

Again with this question. Hadn't her answer last night been sufficient? Kathleen could feel *Mum*'s gaze on her back. "It was very hard work. I never felt as though I was doing things right." Her parents couldn't have issue with that. The truth, yet not encouraging.

Giggling came from down the row Jessica was in.

"What's so funny?" *Mum* asked.

Jessica shook her head.

Kathleen went on. "The professors had particular ways they wanted assignments completed. Other students didn't like it if you got a higher grade than them. Most everyone didn't think I belonged." Most of the time *she* hadn't felt as though she belonged either. In truth, she *hadn't* belonged. *This* was where she belonged, and yet, she felt out of place here as well.

Jessica giggled again.

Mum straightened. "You can't keep all the fun to yourself."

Jessica bit her lip before she spoke. "She has an accent."

Kathleen straightened now. "In *Deutsch*?" She knew she did in English.

Her youngest sister nodded.

She turned to Ruby and *Mum*. Both nodded. Then *Mum* said, "It doesn't matter."

But it did. It would make her stand out. She didn't need more things to give the church leaders reason to question her Amish integrity. Straightening, she determined to eliminate her accent. She'd thought she could easily slip back into this life without effort. Evidently not. Fourteen years *was* a long time to be absent. What else of her Amish life had been whittled away? Had Noah Lambright noticed her accent? Noticed she wasn't completely Amish anymore? Would everyone? She would work extra hard to make sure she once again looked, sounded and acted Amish. And thought like an Amish.

* * *

At midmorning, Noah rode into the Yoders' yard. He wasn't sure why he'd come. He'd just sort of ended up there.

A woman stood in the side yard pounding a stick into the grass with a hammer.

A smile pulled at his mouth.

Kathleen.

She hadn't been a figment of his imagination. He jumped to the ground and tethered his horse. He stood there and watched her.

After tying a string to the top of the stick, she marched with measured steps.

What was she doing?

She pounded another stick into the ground, tied the string around that one, and strode toward a fourth stick already in the ground. Her enclosure was neither a true square nor a rectangle.

He walked over to her. "What are you doing?"

Looking up, she gifted him with a smile. *"Hallo."* She spread her hands out. "This is my clinic."

"You're building it? Yourself?"

"Ja."

"With those string lines?"

"Ja."

How could he tell her she had no clue what

she was doing without hurting her feelings? "And what if you don't get permission from the church leaders?"

"Who says I haven't?"

He folded his arms across his chest. "Have you?"

She hesitated, wiggling her lips back and forth. "*Ne.* But I will. So I want to be prepared."

She had no idea how unprepared she was.

"Have you ever constructed a building before?"

"I went to many barn raisings when I was young. And I earned a medical degree. I don't think putting up a few walls will be that hard. Just nail some boards together. I don't need anything fancy."

Construction was so much harder than she realized. Not so much "hard" as there was a lot more that went into putting up a building than *just nailing some boards together.* He pointed with both index fingers. "Your far *wall* is wider than this one by at least a foot." He indicated the closest string. Probably more, but he was being generous.

She turned and studied the lines. "A foot? That won't really matter once I lay the boards down, will it?"

It would matter. A building needed right angles and straight lines to be sturdy. "You may be able to take out a person's appendix, but you should leave construction to others."

Her blue eyes brightened. "Are you offering to help me?"

"Let's wait and see if you get approval."

"I'll get approved."

He liked her self-assurance. "You're sure?"

She took a deep breath and released it. "One minute, I'm confident they will approve. Or why else would *Gott* have sent me away for so long to become a doctor if not for this?" Her self-assurance held a hint of doubt.

"But?"

Her shoulders drooped slightly. "The next minute, I feel all is hopeless. That I wasted the last fourteen years of my life. Years I could have spent here, with my family."

Her conflict was a valid one. The elders might not give her approval, then the fourteen years would have been for naught. What would she do then? Leave? That thought rankled him. "If *Gott* did send you away for all that time to become a doctor, then pray for Him to make it happen."

"And if it doesn't? What do I do then?"

"Don't make plans for what may not happen. That invites trouble."

"You're right. I should focus on what I have control of. And that's the building for my clinic."

She had less control over that than she imagined.

"Will you help me get my walls straightened out?"

He wasn't sure there was much point but gladly helped her.

After lunch, Kathleen stood at the table rolling out piecrust, her thoughts on Noah and how he'd helped her stake out her clinic. She sensed he believed it might be a waste of time in the end, but that made his lending a hand all that much more sweet. He'd shaved off his beard and looked even more handsome. And available.

Nonsense. She had to stop thinking that way.

The crunch of buggy wheels alerted her that someone had entered the yard. "*Mum*, you have company."

Mum peered out the kitchen window. "*Ne, you* have company."

"Me?" Who would be visiting her? Noah again? Her heart danced at the thought, but it wasn't likely the visitor was him. So who could it be? No one else knew she was back. She covered the partially rolled crust with a damp towel, then tucked the other half of the dough under the corner of the cloth as well to keep them from drying out.

She followed *Mum* through the kitchen doorway outside with Ruby and Jessica tagging along. Her breath caught at the sight of her older sister, Gloria, pulling to a stop.

Mum approached the side where a smiling girl, about ten, sat with a one-year-old on her lap. The baby stretched out his arms, and *Mum* scooped him up. Between the girl and Gloria sat a boy of about four. The girl scooted out and helped the boy down.

Gloria sprang from the buggy and wrapped Kathleen in her arms. "You're home. At long last, you're home." She pulled back to look at her. "You've grown up. I still pictured you as the girl who left. But you've come back a woman." She hugged Kathleen again. "How are you?"

Her older sister was a welcome sight. Even though her family hadn't been allowed to write to her, they all seemed happy to have her home. Kathleen smiled. "I'm *gut*. And you?"

"Wonderful." Gloria turned to her children and pointed to the baby. "This is Luke. He's one. Mark is four. Andrew's with his *vater*. He's six." She paused at the girl. "My oldest is ten. I named her after our sister… Nancy."

Kathleen stared at the girl who looked a lot like their sister. Nancy would have been twenty-

six, but she'd had an allergic reaction to a bee
sting when she was eight. By the time *Dat* had
raced into town at ten miles an hour, she'd suc-
cumbed to anaphylactic shock.

That was the day Kathleen became determined to be a doctor. Nancy had died needlessly because there was no medical care close
at hand.

Kathleen turned to little Nancy. "You look so
much like her. I'm pleased to meet you."

The girl stared up at Kathleen. "*Danki. Mutter* and *Grossmutter* say that too."

Mum waved her hand at Nancy and Mark.
"There are cookies in the kitchen."

The pair ran into the house with Ruby and
Jessica following.

Kathleen turned to Gloria. "Is your Nancy
allergic?"

Gloria hooked her arm through Kathleen's.
"Fortunately, she's never been stung, but Andrew and Mark have. I've feared for her. But
now that you're back, I won't worry so much."

Her sister and the children stayed for a few
hours, then left midafternoon to get home in
time to prepare supper. She would see them all
in two days for the whole community church
services.

After Gloria left, *Mum* brushed her hands

down her apron and sighed. "Time to get started on our supper."

Kathleen stood from where she'd been sitting on the porch, sewing buttons onto the men's shirts for her *mum*. "What can I do to help?"

"You stay put," *Mum* said. "We have it all in hand." The three went inside, leaving her alone.

She eased back into the rocking chair. She wasn't needed. She'd been gone too long. She didn't fit into the daily routine of the household. Should she go inside and insist on helping? *Ne*. For today, she would enjoy this little bit of solitude. And once she had her clinic up and running, she wouldn't be available as much to help. So it might be best if they didn't get used to her helping in the kitchen.

Movement by the barn caught her attention.

A tricolor Australian shepherd sniffed around an old stump. It wasn't just any dog, but Kaleidoscope. She looked around for Noah but didn't see him. A smidge of disappointment pinched at her. "Kaleidoscope! Here, girl!" The dog charged toward her. "You're supposed to be at home."

The Australian shepherd rolled onto her back, curving head to tail, this way then that. Her tail thumping, kicking up dust.

Kathleen crouched and scratched the dog's

belly. She stood and ordered the dog to do the same.

Kaleidoscope flipped to her feet and wagged her tail, causing her whole body to wiggle.

"Come on." Kathleen patted her thigh as she walked around the house to the kitchen door and spoke through the storm door. "Noah Lambright's dog is here again. Do you have a rope so I can walk her back home?"

Mum stood on the other side of the screen. Shaking her head, she reached beside the door and produced a rope. "This is what we usually use to return her. Kaleidoscope, one of these days, we're going to keep you." She opened the storm door and handed Kathleen the rope. "Wait a minute."

Mum disappeared from view, and Kathleen tied the rope around the collar. When *Mum* opened the door, the Aussie raised up on her haunches to receive the tidbit and licked *Mum*'s hand clean.

No wonder the dog kept coming back. She knew where to get treats.

Kathleen started to tell her *mutter* to stop feeding the dog, but a little Amish voice inside her said that was the way they did things here. "I'll be back soon."

Mum called after her. "Invite Noah for supper.

With no one to cook for him, I fear he doesn't eat well."

Noah coming for supper? That sent her insides dancing. "He won't be there, hence the reason for his dog being here."

"There's a key under the rock to the left of the back porch. Write a note and leave it on his table."

Enter someone else's home when they weren't there? The English certainly wouldn't do that. She had much to get used to and relearn.

"All right." Kathleen walked up the driveway with Kaleidoscope happily trotting beside her. She'd seen which way Noah'd left the night before and headed that direction. He'd said his farm was next to her parents'. She found herself smiling at the thought of seeing him again. How silly. She wasn't looking for a husband as most single Amish women were. She couldn't afford to. Not if she was going to succeed at becoming a doctor here.

It didn't take long to get there. His house and that of her parents were both on the sides of their respective properties closest to the other. No wonder Kaleidoscope wandered over so easily. She probably thought their property was part of hers as well.

The house was a typical large home ready for a big family, with an even larger barn as well as a *dawdy haus* for his parents. Did he have one or both of them living in the smaller dwelling? Not likely. *Mum* had said he had no one to cook for him, and he hadn't worried about informing anyone last night when he stayed to supper at their house.

She wished her parents had a *dawdy haus*, then she wouldn't have to build a clinic, but then it might be occupied with her *grosseltern*, which would be nice. Both sets of *grosseltern* lived on her parents' older siblings' properties.

A sleek black shepherd and a small corgi trotted up to her and her detainee, all tails swinging at a different tempo. She petted them each in turn.

If Kathleen had any doubts that this was the right place, they were brushed away with the wagging tails. She untied the rope, feeling it safe to free Kaleidoscope to run with her pals, and walked to the barn. "Noah?"

When she got no answer, she crossed the yard to the big house and knocked on the front door. Still no answer, so she headed around to the back and found the key. She turned it over in her hand. It didn't feel right to walk into someone else's home uninvited. She didn't know Noah well enough. This would be an invasion of his privacy. So she replaced the key and sat in a rocking chair on the front porch, hoping he would return soon.

Some time later, she heard her name being called.

"Kathleen?"

"One more minute." She needed just one more minute of sleep before her shift.

"Kathleen?"

That couldn't be a nurse or orderly. They wouldn't call her by her first name. Where was she? She forced her eyes open and focused on the tall, handsome man standing over her. Not medical personnel. Noah! She smiled, then jerked fully awake. "I'm so sorry. I must have dozed off for a minute." She'd learned to sleep anywhere, and her body knew to catch sleep whenever it could.

"Don't worry." He chuckled. "You weren't snoring."

As she pushed to her feet, the rope on her lap slipped to the porch floor. "I didn't sleep much last night." She was used to taking five-and ten-minute naps throughout the day. No more. She would need to teach herself to sleep at night again and stay awake during the day.

He picked up the makeshift leash and offered it to her. "I must say, the last thing I expected to find when I came home was a pretty lady sleeping on my porch."

She took the rope. "You're not going to let me forget this, are you?"

"Probably not."

His smile did funny things to her stomach. And he'd called her pretty. That didn't matter. She had no room in her life for men. One man in particular. She couldn't have a husband and still be a doctor. She'd made that sacrifice years ago. But still, her heart longed.

She held the lead out and teased him back. "Then maybe next time, we'll keep your dog."

"Kaleidoscope?" He shook his head. "I closed her up in the barn. How did she get out? *Danki* for bringing her back. And because you did, I promise not to mention your afternoon nap."

"*Danki.* I'd appreciate that." Then she remembered her reason for staying. "*Mum* has invited you to supper. Shall I tell her you're coming? Or not?"

"I never pass up an invitation from your *mutter*. Let me hook up the trap, and we can head over."

"What time is it?"

"Nearly supper time. I'll be right back." He jogged to the barn.

How long had she slept? Longer than she'd thought, apparently. She hadn't realized the number of things she'd have to get used to again.

No chance of slipping back into her Amish life as though she'd never been gone.

Noah returned shortly, leading a horse and the two-wheeled trap he had been driving yesterday. "Kaleidoscope dug her way out. I'll need to figure some other way to contain her. Hopefully, she'll stay put in that stall. I gave her plenty of food and water."

Kathleen climbed into the vehicle. He settled in beside her, along with the aromas of wood and honey, and put the trap into motion.

"May I ask you a question? Do you hear an accent when I talk?"

He nodded. "It's slight but comes out on certain words. Nothing to worry about."

"But it is. If the church leaders think I've become too English, they might not accept me back."

"How you talk isn't going to get you thrown out or shunned."

"I need them to accept me as the community's doctor. I can't have anything they can use against me. I went through a lot of trouble to gain special permission to be able to wear my plain dresses and *kapp* instead of scrubs while working in the hospitals."

"You did?" He sounded surprised.

"Though I haven't joined church, I *am* Amish."

He didn't respond. What did his silence

mean? Would everyone meet her declaration of being a doctor for their district and being Amish with silence? She wanted him to approve.

After a moment, he said, "May I ask *you* a question now?"

She smiled.

"Why are you so determined to be a doctor? As you said, you went to a lot of trouble and time away for something that isn't likely to be sanctioned, regardless how you speak."

"I didn't want to leave," she replied. "*Gott* called me to be a doctor. A doctor for our community." She should tell him about Nancy. It would give her practice for speaking to the church leaders.

"My sister was stung by a bee when she was eight. She went into anaphylactic shock. Because medical treatment was too far away, she died before my *dat* could get her to the help she needed. With a simple injection, she would have lived. A simple injection almost anyone could administer."

She hadn't spoken aloud about Nancy in years. Every other time she'd told someone, her eyes flooded with tears and the words lodged in her throat. Not this time. All of her medical training had wrung those emotions out of her. She couldn't help people if she became overwrought.

"I'm sorry about your sister." The sincerity in his tone touched her heart.

"*Danki.* I made a commitment to do all I could to help prevent future senseless deaths."

"I commend you for your determination. So what are you going to do now?"

"I don't know what you mean."

"What's your next step? Other than planning to build a clinic with your own two hands."

"You don't think I can do it?"

"I think your medical degree didn't include a course in construction."

"*Ne*, it didn't. But I think I can manage."

He harrumphed.

"You don't think I'm capable?"

"I think your time would be better spent on other endeavors."

Other endeavors? Like getting married and keeping house and having babies? A longing tugged at her heart. All things she wanted but couldn't have. "I'm going to petition the leadership to give me a trial period. Like they do for testing out the use of new technology in the community. If they can see the benefits for everyone, and people get used to not having to drive all the way into town, then my being the community doctor will be accepted. Then I'll build my clinic that people can come to." She knew in reality that no one would—even if they wanted to—without the leadership's consent. "Until that time, I have my backpack of medical supplies. I'll take it with me wherever I go and help whomever will allow me to."

"Sounds like you have it all figured out."

But she didn't have it all figured out. She still needed to build her clinic. Something she had no clue how to do. Hopefully when she got approval, *Dat* and her brothers would help her. "I've thought about this for over fourteen years. This isn't some fly-by-night thing."

"I can see that."

"I gave up a lot, all those years with our people and more, to learn the skills to help them. I'm going to help our people, whether they like it or not." Then they would see how much they needed her—a doctor in their community—and she would be accepted.

"What about the bishop and church leadership?"

"I'll make them see this is for the *gut* of the community."

"And what if you can't?"

"As you said, don't make plans for what might not happen. I can do this. I know I can. And I'm believing that they are all smart men who will be able to do what is *gut* for everyone." Saying she could convince them and having the actual words that would sway them were two different things. She would go over her arguments for having a clinic and come up with counters for their arguments against. "You probably think all my efforts are going to be wasted, don't you?"

"Let's just say that you have a very steep uphill battle in front of you. And you think more like an *Englisher* than an Amish."

She was afraid of that. And she had an accent to boot. She would talk to *Dat* and *Mum*—when the others weren't around—to straighten out her thinking.

Lord, guide me in what to say and how to get my Amish brothers and sisters to accept me as their doctor. And...let Noah not think poorly of me for my aspirations.

On Saturday, Noah looked up with a start as Bishop Bontrager drove into his yard. He set aside the dog brush and sent Kaleidoscope off, then crossed to the man's buggy as it came to a stop. "I wasn't expecting you."

The bishop didn't get out of his buggy. "I have a favor to ask of you."

"Of course."

"You're close with the Yoders, *ja*?"

"*Ja.*"

"Keep an eye on Kathleen. Let me know if there is anything I need be concerned about."

Spy on Kathleen? "Do you suspect trouble?"

"I don't know. She's been gone a long time. I don't want her stirring things up."

Kind of like Kathleen's plan with being a doctor. Though her intentions weren't to cause trouble but to help. "I'll let you know."

"Danki." Bishop Bontrager drove off.

Noah watched him leave. Should he have told the bishop Kathleen's plans? He didn't feel it was his place at the moment. Kathleen would let the church leaders know her plans soon enough. Tomorrow. For now, he would see how things played out.

The bishop's visit had pulled Kathleen to the forefront of his mind when he'd worked hard to push thoughts of her back. Now with the bishop's request, she would remain front and center. She had to if he was going to keep an eye on her. He liked the idea of keeping an eye on her, but not spying.

Lord, I don't want to spy on her. How can I do as the bishop asks and not feel as though I'm betraying Kathleen or the Yoders?

Chapter Four

The following day, Kathleen climbed out of the buggy last at the Millers' farm. "*Dat*, you'll tell the leaders I wish to speak to them?"

"*Ja*. Don't worry. They'll hear you. But granting you permission will be another issue altogether."

She didn't want to be noticed or singled out. She wanted to blend seamlessly into the throng. But such was not to be the case.

Mum greeted several women who commented on Kathleen's return. Soon a gathering of women crowded around her and her *mutter*. A number of ladies close to Kathleen's age were among the group. She'd gone to school with these girls. Each one had either a small child or two in tow, a baby on their hip or were expecting. Or a combination of the three with older children scattered about. Kathleen wondered what it would be like to be pregnant and have children of her own. But that was not the path the Lord had laid out for her.

Noah popped into her mind, and she sighed. She was a doctor and would be helping each and every one of these women and their children. They all seemed glad to have her back.

Relief swept over Kathleen when people started filing into the house. That was until it was Kathleen's turn to step inside. This was it. She was back.

After a couple of hymns, the bishop stood in front of the community. Bishop Bontrager had been bishop long before Kathleen had left. He was close to the oldest person in their district. "I'm pleased to say that this Sunday is the first class for our young people who want to join church this fall." His voice was still strong. And he still scared her. He was a gruff, strict man. "Those who plan to become church members please stand."

Kathleen stood, pleased she hadn't missed this opportunity. The timing was perfect. The leaders would see she was serious about her faith and returning to the community before she spoke to them of her plans.

Her brother Benjamin stood as well, but not Joshua. He was still young and likely needed another year or two. She was glad Benjamin would be in class with her.

Two others stood as well, a twenty-one-year-old young man and an eighteen-year-old girl and Benjamin, who was twenty. Kathleen, at thirty, felt old. The others were of an average age to join. She tagged along behind everyone following the bishop into the next room. She hadn't wanted to appear pushy, having just returned. She wanted to be respectful of those who had stayed where they belonged.

After eyeing Kathleen for a moment, Bishop Bontrager went over the first three articles of the *Dordrecht Confession of Faith*. These were familiar from her youth. Before long, they rejoined the rest of the congregation.

The church service was so different from the English ones she'd attended while away. At least twice as long, and didn't have the... What was it that was different? Both groups worshipped *Gott*. Both groups sang. Both groups had a message. Maybe the shorter service allowed her to stay focused. And there was an energy among the people. That was it. That's what was different. Which probably had to do with the music. Though the *Englishers* sang hymns, they also sang what they called "praise and worship" songs. Weren't hymns praising and worshipful? They were to Kathleen.

Then there were the instruments. No harmonicas or accordions, and the guitars had been different. They were electric. There was always a keyboard and drums. One church she'd attended had a huge pipe organ. She'd loved to hear it played. She would close her eyes and feel *Gott*'s presence wash over her.

Though she'd enjoyed the diversity in the English churches, she looked forward to the calmer Amish services where she could think and hear *Gott*'s still small voice. The One who had called her away from her people. The One who had sustained her in her studies. The One she couldn't hear now.

She soon learned a bit about Bishop Bontrager's granddaughter who had gone off on *Rumspringa* four years ago and not returned. Kathleen prayed for her.

After service, the bishop excused everyone for their regular cold lunch to be served outside on this sunny day. The bishop called out. "Kathleen Yoder? Please stay behind for a moment."

Her stomach knotted. "Of course." This was it. The church leaders would hear her plead her case.

Dat held back. "Would you like me to stand with you?"

She wanted to say *ja*, but if she was going to stand on her own as a doctor, she would need to show the leadership she could stand on her own now. "I can do this, *Dat. Danki.*" Besides, she didn't want her *dat* to get in trouble for appearing as though he condoned her actions. It had been enough that he'd asked them to grant her an audience.

The church leaders sat in chairs along the front of the room the service had been held in while she stood, facing them. Most she knew because they were the same ones from before she'd left. Once a church leader, always a church leader. Two were new. One of those quite surprising.

Noah Lambright.

Why hadn't he told her he was part of the church leadership? She had gone on and on about being a doctor and helping their community. And stupidly, she'd believed he was interested. Had he been gathering information for the church leaders to use against her? How naive and foolish of her. Was there any point to even pleading her case? She looked from face to stoic face. Were their minds already made up?

No matter. *Gott* had called her, and she would obey, even if the leadership told her *ne*.

Noah gave her a nod. Was that for encouragement? Or an I-told-you-so gesture?

She took several deep breaths while she waited. The bishop cleared his throat. "First, I'd like to say on behalf of the whole church leadership, how pleased we are that you've returned where you belong."

She could hear the "but" coming.

"But you have been away a very long time. You have been involved in things you knew went against the *Ordnung* and what we believe as a people. We fear you have been corrupted by the *Englishers* and their world."

She wanted to interrupt but knew it would be better to remain silent. Something she'd learned in the English world. To hold her tongue. She would have her chance to speak. She hoped. Or maybe they would simply dismiss her.

Noah leaned forward to look at Bishop Bontrager. "Since she hasn't joined church, she's not under the *Ordnung*."

The bishop inclined his head. "True." He focused his piercing gray gaze on her. "We'll hear you out."

Preacher Hochstetler stood abruptly. "What's the point? Our children get all the schooling they need right here. She willfully went against everything we stand for."

Noah spoke up. "She's technically been on *Rumspringa* all these years."

"But she went to college and got a degree to be a doctor." Preacher Hochstetler again. "She had to know that wouldn't be allowed."

"There is nothing against going to college if you aren't a church member," Deacon Zook said.

"But she expects to be a doctor! Here! That can never be!" Preacher Hochstetler slammed his fist onto his opposite palm.

He really needed to calm down.

Noah sat with his head down, shaking it. Was that directed at her? She hoped it was meant for Preacher Hochstetler.

Bishop Bontrager held a hand up. "Please sit back down."

Preacher Hochstetler's face had turned red. He sat and scowled at her.

The bishop went on. "*Danki.* I said we'd hear her out."

"It's a waste of time," Preacher Hochstetler mumbled.

"No more!" The bishop glared at the man. He took several breaths, then turned back to Kathleen. "You have our attention for fifteen minutes. Then you'll leave, and we'll discuss the matter."

Noah gave her an encouraging nod.

Grateful for the chance, she unfolded the piece of paper with her notes.

"What is the reason the children of the Amish don't go to school past eighth grade? Because the jobs they might get could take them away from the community. But that is not the case for me. I went to university and beyond so that I could return to help our people. I never intended, nor do I now intend, to remain in or return to the English world. Many of our men have been forced to take jobs outside our community to support their families because farmland is becoming more scarce."

She took a deep breath and continued. "I became a doctor to come back and help our community. We go to *English* doctors all the time, take *English* medicine, stay in *English* hospitals. But what if we didn't have to go to them for everything? What if the money we pay them could stay in our community? What if we could be less dependent on them?" After all, wasn't that the basis for a lot of the rules in the *Ordnung*? Not being dependent on the outside world. Being as self-sufficient a society as possible. That was getting harder and harder as men were forced to take jobs outside the community to support their families.

"We keep ourselves separated from the outside world. We don't drive their cars. We don't connect to their utilities. We don't go to their churches. So why the connection to their medical facilities? Because we don't have the education to be our own doctors."

She searched each face for support. "When

my sister Nancy was eight, she was stung by a bee. A normal part of being a child. Who here has been stung by a bee?" She paused in hopes that the men would raise their hands.

Only Noah did. But when he realized no one else did, he lowered his. Peer pressure was great in the community. It was one of the ways people were made to conform.

She gave him a tight smile of appreciation. "One percent of children and three percent of adults are allergic to bee stings. My sister was in that one percent. Because treatment was an hour's buggy ride away, she died when a simple injection could have saved her life if gotten to her soon enough. I watched my little sister die. How many others in our community have died needlessly? Women in childbirth? Men with heart attacks? Others with treatable conditions? Don't let pride of adhering to the past allow our people to die when we can prevent it."

Silence hung heavy in the room. Stiflingly so.

She shouldn't have accused them of pride.

The bishop offered a solution. "If you, as an *Englisher*, were to set up a clinic in the midst of our community, our people would be allowed to see you as a doctor."

"An *Englisher*? But I'm Amish."

Bishop Bontrager leaned forward. "Not yet, you're not. You haven't joined church. And when you do—if you do—you will be under the *Ordnung* and must obey the rules, which don't include being a doctor." He folded his arms.

"But I've started the classes. Today. I want to join church. I always planned to join church."

"Then you shouldn't have stayed away so long and done so many things that go against our *Ordnung*."

"So if I join church, I won't be allowed to help our people? I don't understand why not."

Bontrager continued. "If we sanction your behavior, then others will go off and try the same kinds of thing. Then our society will fall apart, and we'll have chaos. *All* our beliefs we've held to for hundreds of years could fall apart if we sanction *your* actions."

"But we all go to *Englisher* doctors. If an *Englisher* doctor converted to Amish, would you let him practice medicine to our people?"

"That would be different."

She could see no difference. "Couldn't you tell our people that I'm allowed to help them, but if anyone else tried to do what I did, they would not be allowed?"

"I'm sorry. That would be like talking out of two sides of the mouth. It would confuse people on right and wrong."

She was sorry too. Maybe they would feel differently if one of their family members or themselves were to need her expertise. She locked gazes with the bishop. "You said you'd discuss this before making a decision."

"That's right. We have all we need from you. *Danki.*"

"In your discussion, keep in mind that you've allowed solar panels and buttons. I'm just asking for the same consideration and chance. A trial period to see if this is *gut* for our community." She knew it was *gut* for the community.

"There's no point in discussing this. She can't be allowed to do this." The ill-tempered preacher's face was red again, and he breathed heavily.

Was he having a heart attack? She rushed forward. "Let me check you."

He thrust out his arm. "Don't touch me."

She froze two feet from the glaring man. She couldn't believe he didn't want help. "Take slow, deep breaths." She took the breaths, willing him to breathe and bring down his obviously elevated blood pressure.

Noah waved her off.

She took a few steps backward.

The bishop motioned toward the door.

She glanced at Noah before she turned and left. She'd said all she could think to say. Any more might kill Preacher Hochstetler.

Why couldn't he accept help? He could be having a stroke or heart attack right now. Would he truly rather die than allow her to assess him? So different from the English world.

Noah left quickly at the conclusion of the meeting to find Kathleen.

Everyone was either gathered around the tables set out with food or seated at the other tables, eating.

He couldn't pick Kathleen out of the crowd. She wasn't among them. Had she gone home? Certainly not. That would be too far to walk.

His *vater* strolled up to him. "You look worried, son. Did you have the dream again?"

Noah took a deep breath to focus on his *vater*. He had had the dream. "How could you tell?"

"When you live with someone their whole life, you can tell. Did you catch up to her this time?"

He meant Noah's *mutter*. *"Ne."* It was always the same, following after his *mutter*, trying to catch her to bring her home. Though the setting changed—the barn, town, Sunday service at someone else's farm—the outcome was always the same. His *mutter* turned a corner and Noah hurried after her. But when he went around the building, she was gone. Always gone.

But this time had been different. His *mutter* still disappeared, but an Amish woman stood with her back to him. He didn't know who she was and stared at her back.

In the beginning, he'd had the dream about his *mutter* every night. Over the years, it had tapered off to once or twice a month. And now thrice in as many nights.

"One of these times, maybe you'll catch her. Ask her that question burning in your heart. Unfortunately, you won't get the answer you seek from your dream." His *vater* walked off.

Noah knew that. Because nowhere in his mind did he know why his *mutter* had left. Maybe that was the reason he could never catch up to her. Maybe the dream was telling him that he would never find the answer to his question. His *vater* seemed as anxious for Noah to catch up to her as Noah was himself.

But his *vater* was right. Noah would never know the answer to his question from his dreams. He needed to stop looking back and focus on the future. But what was before him? Everything he'd cared about was in his past. What lay ahead of him except work and loneliness?

Kathleen.

Kathleen?

Noah pushed the remaining thoughts of his *mutter* out of his head and resumed his search for Kathleen. He caught a glimpse of a red dress on the other side of a huge oak tree trunk on the far side of the yard. He approached. "Why aren't you eating?"

She sucked in a breath as she whirled toward him.

"I'm sorry for startling you."

"I didn't think anyone knew where I was. How is Preacher Hochstetler?"

She was thinking of others rather than herself. Someone who was against her plan to help. Admirable. "He's calmed down. I think he'll be fine."

"He should have his blood pressure checked. I was afraid he was going to have a heart attack or a stroke."

"You really do have a doctor's heart. You truly want to help people."

"Of course I do." She shook her head. "Why didn't you tell me you're part of the church leadership? I feel so foolish going on and on about my dreams of building a clinic and of being a doctor."

"Don't be." He'd liked hearing about her dreams and plans.

"Was that your task? To find out about me and report back to the others?"

He opened his mouth to say *ne* even though that was exactly what the bishop had asked of him, but his words were cut off by a high-pitched scream.

Kathleen rushed past him and headed toward the gathering of people and the sound of wailing. Noah followed close behind.

She pressed into the crowd. "Let me through. I'm a doctor."

People with surprised expressions shifted aside for her.

Noah peered over Kathleen's shoulder.

Martha Phillips knelt beside her nine-year-old son, Isaac, who had a half-inch-diameter stick protruding from his thigh.

The boy thrashed about. "Get it out! Get it out! It hurts! It hurts so much!" He reached for the stick.

Kathleen dropped to her knees and grasped the boy's wrist. "Don't touch it." She turned to her brother Joshua. "Get my medical pack from the buggy."

Joshua looked to his *vater*, who nodded his consent. The young man ran off.

Still holding the boy's wrist, she commanded, "Hold him still."

Simon Phillips jerked his son free from Kathleen's grasp. "Get away from my son."

"I'm a doctor. I can help him."

"*Ne!* Don't touch him," Simon growled. "He's my son, and I'll say what's to be done for him."

Kathleen stared at the man as she withdrew her hands, then spoke in a soft voice. "But I can help him."

She sounded so hurt.

Simon ignored her.

Martha stared at her husband. "What will we do?"

Kathleen seemed to steel her resolve with a deep breath. "Move him very carefully to your buggy and get him into town as fast as you can."

Noah chuckled to himself. She was going to help no matter what.

Simon focused on his son. "This is going to hurt. Be brave."

The boy nodded, tears wetting most of his face.

Simon gripped the stick.

Noah held his breath to brace against the boy's pain.

Kathleen lunged forward. "*Ne!* Don't pull it out. Leave it in. Let a doctor remove it."

Noah held her back by thrusting his arm in front of her. "Stay out of this." He couldn't allow her to go against the *vater*'s wishes for his son.

Simon narrowed his eyes at her, then stared at the stick.

Kathleen tilted her head back to look up at Noah. "Do something."

It wasn't for him to interfere, so he prayed instead. "All we can do now is trust *Gott*."

Kathleen unbuttoned her white apron *Mum* had helped her make and held it out to Martha. "When he pulls the stick out, press this on the wound quickly. Firm pressure."

Martha's hand lifted but went back down when her husband shook his head.

"Please let her take this."

Simon shook his head again and yanked the stick out.

Isaac screamed, then fainted. Blood oozed from the tear in the boy's trousers.

Kathleen shook her apron at Martha. "Take it. Please."

This wasn't right. The boy needed help and Kathleen knew what to do.

Martha knew she must obey her husband, so she removed her own black apron, folded it hastily and pressed it to her son's wound.

Kathleen jerked her head back and forth. "We need something to keep the cloth in place."

Noah removed his suspenders and handed them to Martha. "Tie this around his leg and the apron."

Simon accepted the suspenders and did as Noah instructed. As long as it hadn't been Kathleen to offer the item that was needed, it was all right to accept it. How hypocritical.

Noah accompanied Kathleen as she followed the three men carrying the boy to the Phillipses' buggy, where two other men had hitched up their horse. "Keep pressure on it the whole time. Don't let up."

Martha nodded to Kathleen and climbed into the back of the buggy with her son.

As the buggy pulled away with another one in pursuit, the rest of the people gathered in a huge cluster with bowed heads. Different people called out prayers for Isaac.

Noah prayed silently for the boy and then for Kathleen that she could accept whatever the outcome of today was. That she'd done all she could under the circumstances. He wanted to take her into his arms and let her know everything would be all right. But that would be wholly inappropriate, and he didn't know if everything would be all right. Poor Isaac could die.

And Kathleen's heart would be broken. She would have to live with the knowledge that she could have saved the boy but was refused that opportunity because of pride. He prayed that his people would abandon their pride and allow Kathleen to do what she was trained for.

By late in the afternoon, there was still no word on how Isaac fared. Kathleen helped load her family's dishes into their buggy.

Noah approached her *vater*. "Your buggy's already full. May I take Kathleen in mine?"

Dat stilled his hands from hitching up the horse.

Kathleen willed her *dat* to say *ne*. She didn't want to sit in Noah's buggy. Not after learning of his deception.

She shook her head.

Dat said, "You'll take her straight home?"

"*Ja*. We'll travel directly in front of you."

"Very well," *Dat* said.

Noah escorted her to his waiting buggy, keeping one hand on the waist of his suspenderless trousers. Though *Englishers* rarely ever wore them, she'd already gotten used to the Amish men wearing them. So, to see Noah without his looked odd.

She climbed into his open two-wheeled trap without his help. Did he not have a proper enclosed buggy? "I would have preferred to ride with my family."

He settled in beside her and took up the reins. "I could tell."

"Then why force me to ride with you?"

"I need to talk to you."

"Why didn't you tell me? About being part of the leadership?"

He clucked the horse into motion. "I never really thought about it. Everyone knows who the church leaders are, so I don't go around announcing it to everyone I come in contact with. It never crossed my mind you didn't know. But now that I think about it, unless your parents told you, you wouldn't know. And they obviously hadn't told you."

He was right. Her parents could have told her. But that wasn't something people talked about. And she had been back for only a few days. "I suppose it's reasonable that it wouldn't have come up."

"So am I forgiven?" He turned onto the road.

She knew *Englishers* who withheld forgiveness for weeks, months or even years. She didn't want to freely forgive, but harboring animosity wasn't the Amish way. "Forgiven."

"*Danki.* You asked if I had been tasked with garnering information from you."

That had been the worst of finding out his position. "I don't want to know. I feel foolish enough."

"Though the bishop asked me to keep an eye on you, he didn't ask me to find out about you."

"Isn't that the same thing?"

"I don't believe so. Finding out about you would be to gather information and report back to him. Keeping an eye on you was just that. Seeing that your transition home wasn't complicated."

That surprisingly made her feel better.

"It was *Gott* who set me on the road that day you were walking home. I was intrigued when I found out you were Kathleen Yoder. I couldn't imagine any Amish man—let alone a woman—doing what you did."

He seemed impressed. At least she had that.

"Though I wasn't tasked to get information on you, I have been tasked to tell you the outcome of the leadership."

"Don't bother. I can guess what they decided. When one nearly kills one of the members, the answer is a given." She would have to figure out a different way to help her people. One that didn't strictly go against the leadership. A way that people felt they could come to her for help without being disobedient.

"Because you told me of your hopes and dreams of being a doctor to our community and helping people, I was able to convince the others to allow you to set up a clinic through the summer until you join church in the fall."

"Of course—" She jerked toward him. "What? You did?"

He nodded.

She couldn't believe it. They had approved. She would have liked the trial period to be longer, at least a year, but she'd take what she could get. She sighed. A clinic of her own. Then reality set in. "That doesn't give me much time to build my clinic." If she had help, it could be done in no time. However, if she had to do all the work herself, her trial would be over before she was even finished. Therefore, their approval might mean nothing.

"I have a *dawdy haus* sitting empty."

Had she understood his meaning correctly? "You would let me use it?"

"*Ja.* And setting up on the property of a leader will let people know you have permission. They are more likely to come to you."

Kathleen couldn't believe this. She was going to get her clinic after all, and much sooner than she'd anticipated. "Because you're the one who convinced them to give me a chance, did you *have* to offer your *dawdy haus*?"

"The opposite. Because I offered the place, they agreed to the trial. But you are not to treat anyone nor their children without their consent."

She could abide by that. People would soon see the benefits to her helping them. "Why are you doing this for me? You hardly know me."

He was silent for a minute. "Since my wife and daughter died in childbirth, I've often wondered if I'd called for an ambulance sooner when the midwives first suspected there might be a problem, if my family would have lived. If there had been a trained doctor close at hand, would they have lived? If I'd driven her to the hospital as soon as her labor started, would they have lived?"

Kathleen's heart ached. She didn't want to know the cause of death, because then she would know if there might have been a possibility to save them. And if she knew, she would feel obligated to tell him. He didn't need to carry around the kind of heartache and burden she did for her sister. "I'm so, so sorry for your loss. No words ever make the ache go completely away."

"Most people don't understand that. They go on as though nothing happened and that person never lived to begin with. That hurts as much as their absence."

He understood. He truly understood. How many others who had suffered losses needed someone to tell them that they truly understood? Instead of words of platitudes to placate the grieving.

"Life never goes back to normal. You have to discover a new kind of normal. One that never feels quite right without your loved one. A new way of going about living with part of you missing."

"No one else understands that." He turned into her driveway.

Home already? "I think maybe some people do, but we Amish don't talk about it because we either think we're not supposed to, or more often, we don't know how."

"What time shall I come by in the morning to pick you up?"

"Pick me up for what?" Had she agreed to go somewhere with him and forgotten?

"So you can get set up in the *dawdy haus*."

"I'll walk over. Let me talk to *Dat* and *Mum* about it first."

"I'll tell them so I can let your *vater* know the leadership's decision." He tethered the horse and walked her inside.

All too soon, he left. During the short buggy ride home, she'd gone from not wanting to be near Noah, to not wanting to be parted from him.

It was a *gut* feeling. But was it wise?

Chapter Five

The following morning, Kathleen gathered her medical pack and the basket of baked goods *Mum* was sending to Noah. The man would never go hungry so long as her *mutter* was near. She trekked the half mile next door. An excitement danced through her at the prospect of seeing Noah again so soon. What was she thinking? The excitement must be for setting up her clinic. But no doubt about it, seeing Noah was exciting too.

He'd phoned later last night to let them know that Isaac Phillips's leg was stitched up, and he'd returned home. That had relieved Kathleen's apprehension over the boy's injury and allowed her to sleep. For nearly a full five hours.

Though she didn't see Noah in the yard, Kaleidoscope bounded up, scattering chickens, and flipped to her back, wiggling from side to side. Kathleen scratched the dog's tummy. The other two dogs quickly joined their young pal, so she gave them attention as well. But where was Noah? Disappointment sank inside her that he wasn't there to greet her.

Giving each dog one last pet, Kathleen laughed. "All right. Enough." She stood. "I have work to do."

The dogs scampered off but not far.

She should go to the house to locate Noah first, but eagerness to see her soon-to-be clinic sent her toward the *dawdy haus*. She crossed the yard and onto the porch with her three new friends tagging along, tails wagging. Her clinic would be up and running in no time, and she would soon have patients flooding to see her. As well as having chairs inside, she would line the porch with them so her patients could wait out in the fresh air.

The little sunshine-yellow house had solar panels on the roof. *Gut*. There would be electricity. Maybe she could talk Noah into letting her install a telephone. Then people could call so she could go to them if they couldn't come to her. People shouldn't have to go without medical treatment because they couldn't travel to her. House calls were a thing of the past in the *Eng-*

lisher world. But not so for her Amish brethren. She would need to get herself a buggy.

Stepping up to the door, she peered in the window.

Noah's smiling face appeared on the other side of the glass.

With a gasp, she jerked back. That hadn't been expected.

Noah opened the door. "*Guten Morgen.* You're here. Come in."

She stared at him for a moment before stepping inside the typical *dawdy haus*. A love seat sofa and a couple of recliner rocking chairs occupied the living room that was open to the dining area, which was part of the kitchen. She would need to rearrange things to be more suitable for a doctor's office waiting room. But she wanted to keep the homey feel rather than an institutional one. Over all, it would work nicely.

He took her medical pack and set it on the kitchen table. He gazed at the basket. "What's that?"

Kathleen smiled and held out the basket. "My *mum* sent you some food. She seems to think you never eat unless she cooks for you."

He smiled. "I must admit she cooks a whole lot better than I do."

Of course, being on his own, he had to do all

his own cooking. He had no one to help him. "How many other rooms are there?"

"A bathroom, pantry and two bedrooms. One is quite small."

"That will be perfect." One could be her examination room and the other her office to keep supplies and records locked up in.

"Let me know what furniture you want moved out as well as what else you might need."

She hadn't thought until now what she might need beyond what was in her medical pack. First, what to use for an examination table. One of the beds would be too low and a table, though high enough, wouldn't be long enough.

He interrupted her planning. "What are you thinking?"

She turned to him. "Trying to decide what to use for an examination table."

"I can build you a long, narrow table. Just give me the dimensions."

How thoughtful of him to ask. "I want it about this high. And this long."

He blinked at her as though waiting for her to say more.

"What?"

"The numbers. I can't build something with only *this high* and *this long* to go by. I need measurements."

"I don't know. How high is this?" She held her hand about hip high.

He unclipped a measuring tape from the waist of his trousers. "How high again?" She held up her hand while he measured.

When he clipped the tape measure back onto the waist of his trousers, she asked, "Aren't you going to write down the numbers?"

"*Ne.* I've got them."

Interesting. It was probably like her remembering medication dosages.

His face suddenly brightened. "Hold on. I have something for you. I'll be right back." He left.

He would build her a table? He was already doing so much. Why hadn't she considered all the equipment and supplies she would need in her doctor's office? The clinics she'd worked in had all the equipment and supplies already. She always pictured her clinic fully stocked but had no idea how it all got there. Most things would need to wait.

Returning, he held a three-foot by one-foot board. "It's not finished. It still needs to be stained and the letters painted."

He flipped the board around. Carved into the oak was *The DR. KATHLEEN Clinic.*

She touched it gingerly. "You carved this for me?"

"Ja."

She gazed at him in appreciation. He must have been a fine husband to his wife. And he'd make another woman a fine husband in the future.

Her parents knew him well and liked him. Her brothers and sisters treated him like a brother, not just a spiritual one but an earthly brother as well.

She needed to stop looking at him with eyes that might want more than friendship. For he could never be anything more than a friend to her. She would never have a husband. The thought saddened her. Moreover, thinking of him with a wife felt as though the stick that had stabbed Isaac in the leg was jammed in her chest.

"When did you do this? The leaders decided only yesterday."

"Last night. With no one else here, I have a lot of spare time. I like to keep busy in the evenings so I don't think about…things I shouldn't."

"Oh, don't ever feel as though it's wrong to remember your wife and child. Even though gone from this world, they're still a part of you."

He shifted from one foot to the other.

She'd made him uncomfortable talking about his lost family.

He tipped the sign back and forth. "Do you like it?"

How touching. "It's beautiful. I can't believe you made this for me."

"People need to know this is an official clinic. And that they can start coming by. What else are you going to need to open your clinic?"

"I could come up with a whole list of things. But I'll have to get by with what I have in my pack for now."

"Make a list of everything you might need, and I'll see what I can gather up."

"You don't have to do that. You've already done so much." His kindness and generosity touched her deeply.

"If your clinic is going to be a success, it needs to look like a clinic and be able to meet people's needs." He opened a drawer and pulled out a legal pad and pen. He set them on the table and pulled out a chair. "Write down as many things as you can think of, and while we rearrange things, you can add to it."

"You're going to help me move stuff around?"

"I certainly don't expect you to move the furniture by yourself."

"That's so nice of you."

"Well… I… It's my reputation on the line too. If your clinic doesn't do well, it will be a very long time before I would be able to convince the others to consider anything new."

She hadn't thought about what this meant for him by standing up for her. If she failed, would the others shun him? "If this could get you in trouble, maybe I should find somewhere else."

"Nonsense. I've already committed this place. If you back out now, it would be the same as admitting defeat and failing."

"I never meant to put you in jeopardy, only myself."

"You didn't put me in jeopardy. I volunteered."

She stared at him in disbelief.

"If your being a doctor here can prevent a tragedy like Rachel and our baby's or like your sister, then this will all be worth it. You didn't endure the hardship of being away for fourteen years and working your way through medical school to give up now, did you?"

She shook her head.

"You're going to face a lot more opposition than you did yesterday before you're accepted as a doctor here."

More opposition? "But the leadership approved this. Didn't they?"

"*Ja*, but that won't stop some from discouraging others not to come to you or allow you to treat their families."

This wasn't going to be a simple trial period where people would come and test out having a doctor close at hand. She was going to have to endure the ridicule and scathing glares like she did in medical school and her residencies. Her battle was far from over. She'd thought the hardest part was behind her, but maybe it had just begun.

"Now, sit and make your list."

She sat and wrote down *chairs*. Then she looked at the living room to see how many she thought she should add there. Then she pictured the porch lined with chairs. She wouldn't need the porch *lined* with them. Three or four should be sufficient. In truth, for the number of people who would actually come, just the chairs she could fit in the living room would be sufficient. If she was honest with herself, the current furniture in the living room would be sufficient. With seats to spare.

Was there even any point? Why do all the rearranging and setting up of the clinic if no one would come? It could be a lot of work for nothing.

She stared at the mostly blank yellow paper, overwhelmed by the simple task and everything associated with it.

Noah glanced down at the paper. "Chairs. How many?"

She felt like saying zero but didn't want Noah to know how discouraged she was. "These four table chairs should be enough to add to the living room."

"What about the porch? People might like to wait outside when it's nice."

Matching up in their thinking made her heart happy.

"That would be nice. If you have any extra. But if not, that's fine. I'm sure what's in the living room will be sufficient at first."

He nodded. "What else?"

She didn't even want to think of it all. "Well, the only other things, you wouldn't be able to get."

"Like what?"

"Medical supplies."

He pointed to the paper. "Write them all down so we can work on getting them." When she hesitated, he said, "Write down exam table. Then when I have it done, you can check it off. It always feels *gut*, like you've accomplished something, when you can check it off a list."

She wrote down exam table, sheets to cover it with for each new patient, tongue depressors, gauze, file folders for patient records...

With each new item, she thought of two more. The list became easier and easier to build.

* * *

Noah took her list. Most items would need to be purchased. He hitched up his larger covered buggy and drove Kathleen into town.

He liked working alongside her. Not only was she intelligent, but she wasn't looking at him as a potential husband. Too many of the young women hoped he would court them. He'd had a few *vaters* approach him and young ladies who weren't as subtle as they might have thought they were being. Even the others in the church leadership had come right out and said he needed to marry again. But unless *Gott* directed him to take another wife or the leadership *ordered* him to, he would remain contentedly single. He'd had enough pain to last him a lifetime.

So working with Kathleen suited him fine. More than suited him. It pleased him.

In town, he parked near the chain drugstore. It was large enough to have most of the nonprescription items they needed: gauze, tape, Band-Aids, over-the-counter medications, tongue depressors and such. She could get small quantities to start out with, then order more online. He didn't know what the procedure was for a doctor to order controlled medications, but Kathleen would know. He helped her out of the buggy.

Then he saw the woman at the end of the block watching him. The woman from his dream. His *mutter*.

She ducked her head and disappeared around the corner.

How many times had he seen her in town and ignored her? Unlike in his dream, he always pretended she wasn't there. Never pursued her in real life. However, this time, he had the impulse to go after her. Keeping his attention on the corner, he spoke to Kathleen. "I have something I need to do. I'll meet you inside." He took off down the street.

From behind him, Kathleen said weakly, "All right."

He hurried to the corner.

Gone.

Just like in his dream. He glanced around but couldn't see her anywhere. Probably for the best. What would he have said if he'd caught up to her? He headed back and entered the drugstore.

Kathleen's arms brimmed with supplies.

He grabbed a cart and met up with her. "Put them in."

She dropped them into the cart. "*Danki*. I can't get very much, so I thought I could carry it all. I'm ready to go pay."

He stared into the cart. One roll of gauze, one

of bandage tape, a box of Band-Aids, one bottle of rubbing alcohol, one of hydrogen peroxide, some antibiotic ointment and a bottle of ibuprofen. "You need more than this to run a clinic."

"That's all I can get today."

Meaning that was all she could afford. "I'll buy what you need."

She shook her head. "I couldn't let you do that. I have some supplies in my pack."

Not enough to run a clinic. He could stand here and argue with her, or he could use the time more wisely by filling the cart. He grabbed duplicates of most of the items she already had and several things she didn't.

"What are you doing?" she asked.

"Shopping." He went down another aisle and added several more items.

She stopped in front of the cart and put a hand on it. Her steady blue eyes locked on his. "I know what you're doing. I can't let you buy all this for my clinic. You have already done so much. I will not take advantage of your kindness and generosity."

He had the urge to just stare at her but knew he shouldn't, so he took a slow breath before replying. "You are not taking advantage of me. Think of this as me investing in the future of our district."

"But—"

"You can't actually stop me." He smiled. "Let me do this." It would make up for allowing her to think he was helping her to spare his own reputation. In reality, he *wanted* to help her succeed. Something deep inside him *needed* to help her.

She sputtered several incoherent syllables before ceasing and drooping her shoulders in defeat. She was more beautiful than ever, standing there all flustered.

He paid for everything, even the items she'd put in first.

Out at his buggy, he glanced around for the woman again. He didn't see her.

He took Kathleen to a couple other stores and a medical supply store so she could establish relationships with them.

On the ride home, Kathleen twisted her hands in her lap. "*Danki* for all the supplies. I feel foolish having to accept so much help. If you need any medical treatment, it'll be on the house. You never have to pay for any visits."

"I'm glad to help." Very glad.

It did his heart *gut* to be doing something for someone else. Not because he had to, like a barn raising or because the bishop asked him to—he was always glad to help—but because he *didn't* have to. This was completely voluntary.

Kathleen deserved someone on her side. And he wanted to be that person.

Chapter Six

Later in the week, Noah entered the *dawdy haus*. Grunting noises came from one of the bedrooms. What was going on? He went to investigate and couldn't have anticipated the scene he would find.

Kathleen stood with the mattress on end, wrestling with it. The mattress swayed this way and that. *"Ne, ne, ne,"* she muttered. "Don't be so difficult."

What took place next happened fast. The mattress seemed to heave itself in an attempt to throw Kathleen to the floor and pin her there.

"Whoa! Oh, *ne!*" One of Kathleen's feet lifted as though to balance herself and the mattress, but her effort failed.

Noah rushed into the room, grabbed the mattress and leaned it back on its end against the bed frame.

Kathleen tottered with the absence of the weight.

Noah gripped her arm to steady her. "Are you all right?"

"Ja." She breathed heavily from her battle. *"Danki.* I thought it was going to trap me."

No wonder. She was so small. The mattress probably weighed more than her. What had she been thinking?

"You should have waited for me."

"I thought I could slide it into the other room."

He realized he still held on to her arm. He should let go but didn't want to.

Her eyes widened. *"Ne!"*

Before he could ask what the problem was now, something soft and large struck from behind, falling against him. The mattress. It pushed him forward, and he in turn pushed Kathleen backward. He threw out his hands to keep from crushing her against the wall, and his palms smacked the solid surface. His face lingered inches from hers.

He didn't move.

She didn't move.

Each stared at the other. Oddly, he didn't feel uncomfortable with the closeness. She didn't seem to either. Her blue eyes studied him.

And he studied her. He should probably move but made no effort to do so. She also made no effort to get out of this awkward, compromising situation.

Then all of a sudden, giggles burst out of her. A sweet tingling sound that warmed him and sent shivers over his skin. Kathleen should laugh often.

He had to laugh too. "What's so funny?"

She pointed behind him. "This mattress seems to have a mind of its own."

"So it does."

"I thought it was just being difficult for me, and had something against me. But it seems you have fared no better with it."

"*Ne*, I haven't." But he *had* fared very well at being so near to her. If the mattress were a person, he would need to thank it for creating such a predicament. He really should move now. Standing this close any longer would soon become awkward. He gazed at her like a man who might contemplate marrying again. Which *he* definitely would not. Ever. No matter how many times the church leaders brought up the subject. He wouldn't put himself through that kind of pain again. He knew men who had been widowed two and three times and still married again. He could never do that. Could he?

He pushed against the mattress with his back and removed one hand from the wall. "I'll let you get clear before I attempt to move this thing."

She laughed again. She definitely needed to do that more. She scooted out of the way.

But she seemed like she was reluctant to do so.

He gave the mattress a shove at the same time he spun around to catch it. Gripping the sides, he hoisted it up and carried it into the living room. "Would you get the door?"

Kathleen did. "Where are you taking that to?"

"The big house. I'll store it in one of the rooms there. Unless you want it in the other bedroom in case someone is ill and needs to lie down."

She shook her head. "I doubt a bed would fit. The other room will be my exam room. With the table, supplies and people in there, it will be stuffed. So to the big house it is. I'll go with you and open the front door."

That wasn't necessary. He could easily enough lower the mattress and then pick it up again. However, he wasn't about to turn her down. "Lead the way."

Outside the *dawdy haus*, he hoisted the mattress onto his head and balanced it there. He watched Kathleen stroll across the yard in front of him, all three dogs at her heels. Such a tiny woman. She ascended the porch steps as though she were floating. How did she do that? She opened his front door and moved aside.

"Danki." He shifted the mattress down and entered. He didn't want her to leave and go back to the *dawdy haus* without him. "Would you get the one upstairs?"

"Ja." She slipped in and trotted up to the second floor.

He followed.

"Which room?"

"The last one on the right."

She opened it, then stepped back out of his way.

When he set the mattress against the wall and turned around, his heart sank. She'd left. Probably gone back. But when he went downstairs, he found her waiting by the open front door.

She gazed at him expectantly. "Would you help me with the mattress in the other room?"

He smiled. "Of course. And with the frames. And any other furniture you need removed from the *dawdy haus*." He'd gladly help her all day if she needed him to.

After a long morning of moving furniture, Kathleen went about scrubbing the house, top to bottom. She needed a fairly sterile environment.

Noah had gone about his farm chores. She missed his presence. He'd been absent for the last hour. A couple of times when she peeked out the window, she saw him on a ladder against his house. She couldn't figure out what he'd been fiddling with. She had to stop looking for him and wondering where he was every minute.

A thump on the outside of the *dawdy haus* startled her. Then a drill boring into the siding. The sound of electrical tools and appliances still sounded odd. She wasn't sure she liked them. So much noise.

She laughed to herself. Compared to the *Englisher* world, this was silence. Never a moment's peace in the outside world. She'd fondly anticipated returning to the quiet of her community. But she did like electricity. She couldn't have it both ways.

She could understand why some Amish resisted new things and change. Electricity meant more noise and a faster pace of life. She hadn't felt as though she'd gotten to slow down to the previous leisurely pace of life from before she left. She supposed that was gone. Gone forever. How sad. A part of her longed to have the unhurriedness back. But would she be willing to sacrifice electricity to have it? Probably not, now that it was here.

Noah came inside and nodded to her.

She caught herself smiling at him. "What are you doing?"

He gave her half of a smile in return. "You'll see. No peeking." He pointed. "Wait on the porch."

She folded her arms. "Are you kicking me out of my own clinic?"

He folded his arms with a cordless drill in one hand and a screwdriver in the other. "Your clinic, but my *dawdy haus*. Do you want a surprise or not?"

She did. He seemed almost giddy with his secret. "Will it take long?"

"If you keep detaining me? *Ja*."

She huffed a breath and stepped out onto the porch. What could it possibly be?

The dogs lay sprawled in the shade on the porch. Kaleidoscope lifted her head but didn't get up. The other two only rolled their eyes in her direction. All three probably wondered if it would be worth the effort to get up on the off chance she would pet them. Maybe later.

She settled into the rocking chair Noah had brought over from the big house's porch. She could use a break anyway. Leaning her head back, she put the chair into motion and relaxed into it.

"Kathleen?"

She forced her eyes open. Again? She'd fallen asleep again? She needed to stop sitting down on his porches. They lulled her to sleep faster than anything. *"Ja."*

"It's ready."

She stood. "How long was I asleep this time?"

He shrugged. "Twenty minutes maybe. How is it you can fall asleep anywhere?"

She explained the long work hours at the hospital. "I learned to grab sleep when I could. Often several five-and ten-minute naps throughout the day."

He shook his head. "I can't imagine living like that."

"I couldn't either until I was. It's amazing what the human body will adapt to. I'm trying hard to adjust back to normal sleeping habits, but my brain is resistant to accepting that this is the new way of life." She clapped her hands and rubbed them together. "So…what's this surprise?"

He motioned with his hand toward the door. "Come see."

The dogs jumped to their feet and wiggled over, tails wagging.

"You three stay outside." He led Kathleen inside and back to the smaller of the two rooms, the one she'd designated for her office. "Notice anything different?"

She scanned the empty room and spied it immediately on the floor below the window. "A phone." She turned to him. "You installed a phone." A cordless phone.

"It's just an extension of the one I have in the house and barn, so it's the same number. But no one usually calls me, so you can tell people that during the day, they can reach you here."

"I love it." She stepped forward and started to give him a hug but stopped herself. Not the Amish thing to do. She'd gotten used to people hugging her in the outside world. Even men. Men hugged women and vice versa. It was a way of greeting each other. But not for the Amish. She would need to retrain herself. "*Danki. Danki* very much."

"I figured it would help with you getting patients and communicating with them."

"*Ja*, it will. You have been very thoughtful."

"The other handset is in the kitchen area."

"Two phones. Is that a little extravagant?"

He chuckled. "I have a desk in the house I don't use that I'll bring out, and I can build you a bookshelf along that wall if that'll be helpful."

"Both of those would be wonderful, but I don't want to trouble you."

"It's no trouble."

She knew it was. How could it not be?

"I'll be right back."

"Back? Back from where?"

"The house to retrieve the desk." And with that, he left.

"Should I help?" she called after him.

"*Ne*, I can get it," he called back.

She liked his consideration and helpfulness.

Not everyone would be so accepting of her being a doctor. Most people probably wouldn't until the leaders gave their full approval.

He returned a few minutes later, hefting a smallish desk in front of him by one end.

How was he managing by himself?

He set the desk down and plunked the phone on top of it. "It's starting to look like a real office in here."

It certainly was.

He left the room and returned with a kitchen chair that he set behind the desk. "Try it out."

She sat and ran her hands across the surface. A long, shallow top drawer ran the width. On either side of her chair were two more of medium depth, and the bottom ones on each side were file-folder depth. She could keep all her records in those.

Though the lines were in a simple Amish style, it was a refreshing change from the industrial metal or ornate wood *Englisher* desks. "It's perfect." She would need to get a computer at some point for both record keeping and researching. That is, if the church leaders would approve it. And a copier-printer. Before she bought anything more, she needed to prove her worth as a doctor.

"So it'll work for you?"

"Oh, *ja*. It's beautiful."

A smile pulled at his mouth. *"Danki."*

She tilted her head. Something in his tone made her wonder. "Did you make this?"

"Ja." His smile widened.

He had a nice smile. Engaging. She wanted to study it as she might a virus under a microscope, cataloging every detail, including the causes as well as the effects.

"Would you like to see my workshop in the barn?"

"Ja, I would." She stood and walked to the barn with him.

The dogs got up from where they lay in the grass and trotted along with them.

The scent of cut wood hung strong in the air. And no wonder, the workshop wasn't just *in* the barn, it took up most of the building. Rows of finished straight-back chairs, dining tables, rocking chairs, benches, porch bench swings, headboards and footboards, dressers, and even wooden spoons and toys. If it was made out of wood, Kathleen suspected it could be found in here. She could tell this was where his heart lay. "Why do I smell honey? And…linseed oil?"

"You have a *gut* nose. I don't use chemical-based finishes. I make my own boiled linseed oil as well as a beeswax furniture wax."

The source of him always smelling so *gut* and sweet.

He ran his hand over a piece. "It's not as durable as polyurethane or varnish, but I like to keep the finish more natural. I feel the chemical finishes smother the wood. Wood needs to breathe."

His pieces were beautiful and smelled fresh.

She pointed toward the door. "I thought the surrounding fields were yours."

"They are. I rent them out to one of the Zook families."

"What about your sheep? Isn't that why you have dogs?"

"I have dogs because I like them. They're *gut* company." He dipped his head. "The sheep were my wife's idea. She wanted to spin her own wool. I have no interest in that. The Troyers shear them and pay me a moderate price for the wool. I should just sell the animals to them. But then what excuse could I have for keeping my dogs?"

She laughed. "Because you want to."

"Come over here." He walked to what appeared to be his work area and pointed to a pile of finished boards. "These will be your bookshelves."

She ran her hand over the smooth wood. "Really?"

He nodded. "I'll put them together tomorrow inside."

She looked more closely. Holes were drilled in the ends of the boards and a pile of wooden dowel pins sat nearby.

"I need you to approve your exam table." He motioned toward a piece of furniture, then lifted one half of the surface that seemed to have a hinge in the middle. "This is so you can sit the patient up if you need to, like I've seen in doctors' offices."

Not the flat piece of wood with legs she'd envisioned. "And drawers underneath for storage."

He nodded. "See if it's the height you wanted."

Standing next to it, she ran her hands across the surface. She would need to sew a thin mattress to cushion the surface. But other than that, she couldn't ask for anything nicer. "It's perfect. You didn't have to go to all this trouble."

"I wanted to. It's nice to have someone appreciate my work."

"What do you do with all your pieces?"

"Nothing yet. Now that I have some stock, I'm trying to decide if I want to have a store in town or set up a website."

"You could do both. These will fetch a fine price in the *Englisher* market. You could set your shop up right here on your farm." Then he wouldn't be so far away during the day.

"I've thought of that. It's one of my many business decisions. Fortunately, I make enough from renting out my fields to be able to take my time."

"Don't forget the sale of your wool."

He smiled again. "That only covers feeding and housing the sheep. I really should just sell them to the Troyers."

"That would leave you more time for the work you love."

His face brightened.

She smiled in return. *Ja*, a closer study of his smile would be interesting. For now, she should get back to work.

Chapter Seven

Two days later, as Kathleen headed out the door to go to her clinic, she wondered if Noah'd had time to install the bookshelves. He did have livestock to tend to and work to do around his place. He couldn't be expected to wait on her. She'd missed seeing him yesterday, having stayed home to help inventory the pantry and cellar.

Jessica trotted up to her but called back to their *mum* in the kitchen. "Can I go with Kathleen and help out at her clinic?"

Mum came toward them at the front door with a basket in her hands. "I don't want you to be in the way. You don't know any medical stuff. What would you do all day?"

"Oh, answer the telephone and check in the patients and anything else she needs me to do." Jessica turned to Kathleen. "Right?"

"Sure." If the phone rang at all, Jessica was

welcome to answer it, and if any patients came, she could certainly greet them. The idea of her sister working with her appealed to her. More likely, Jessica would have nothing to do all day, but the company would be nice.

"That's fine then." *Mum* handed Kathleen the basket. "There should be enough in there for three. Invite Noah for supper."

"Three?" Kathleen said.

"You, Noah and now Jessica. Have a *gut* day, you two." She returned to the kitchen.

Jessica slung a cloth bag over her shoulder. Evidently, she had packed herself a few things for a day away.

Once out on the porch, Kathleen turned to her baby sister. Well, she wasn't so young anymore. She would start *Rumspringa* next summer. "I don't want to give you false hope, but I haven't had a single patient, and no one knows to call, so there won't be anything to do all day. You'll likely get very bored. Don't get me wrong, I'd love to have your company. I just don't want to mislead you into thinking this will be some exciting adventure." Though getting to know her sister as nearly a grown-up would be a blessing. She'd missed so much of Jessica's life.

"Oh, don't worry about any of that. If I get bored, I have a book to read in my bag as well as some sewing. I mostly wanted to spend time with you and get to know my big sister. And to get out of a little work around here at home." Jessica gave a winning smile. "I won't be in your way. I promise."

Kathleen looped her arm through Jessica's. "I welcome your company." She was thrilled that they had the same intentions—to get to know each other. Apparently, some of the attachment they'd shared all those years ago still remained.

Arm in arm, they walked up the driveway. Kathleen said, "Do you have your eye on a special young man? One you hope might ask to court you?"

"*Ne.* I'm not interested in boys yet. I have more important things on my mind. Tell me about college. What kinds of things can you study?"

"Why do you want to know about that?" It would be irresponsible to encourage her sister in this.

"I want to go like you did."

How could she dissuade her sister? "Do you think college is all fun?"

Jessica shook her head. "*Ne.* I think, like you, I would not like it."

"Then why would you want to go?"

"I feel *Gott* calling me to go to college, like He did you."

Kathleen couldn't help but feel as though her

sister was saying that because that had been Kathleen's excuse as well. Though, *Gott had* called Kathleen. But she'd tried to persuade Him otherwise. "Have you told *Dat* and *Mum* this?"

"*Ne.* They would tell me not to."

"As I must do. I don't think you should consider college for one more minute."

"But you went. Just tell me about it. Then maybe I can tell if I'm truly supposed to go. Some days I think I'm supposed to, and others it scares me."

It *should* scare her.

"I wouldn't be gone nearly as long as you were."

Kathleen supposed she'd have to have this discussion eventually if Jessica was determined. If not today, then tomorrow or next week or next month. "I went with a purpose. You don't go to college just to take whatever classes you want." Well, technically she could. "You have to study in a particular area. What would you study?"

Jessica didn't hesitate. "Business."

"Business? For what?"

"I think it would be *gut* for me to know about how to run a business. To make the most of all we do here as Amish. *Englishers* love everything Amish. I don't know if I want to run my own business someday or to help other Amish with their businesses. We could do so much more if we knew how to utilize computers and the internet better. Amish once could do quite well separated from the *Englisher* world, but not so much anymore. We grow food to make them dependent on us, but it also makes us dependent on them. Computers are no different."

Her sister sounded a bit like an *Englisher* herself. "How would you even pay for tuition? It's not free."

"The same way you did."

"It's not that easy. I had a nurse who mentored me and helped me out a great deal. She gave me books and found scholarships and so much more. Without her, I couldn't have done it."

"I'll find someone to help me too. If *Gott* wants me to go, then He'll provide the means."

Kathleen had to talk her sister out of this. Her parents would be angry and blame her. Even though she had nothing to do with it.

By the time they'd concluded the short walk to Noah's, she had still been unsuccessful in dissuading Jessica. A part of her was proud of her baby sister.

Suddenly, Kaleidoscope dashed from around the house to greet them.

Inside the *dawdy haus*, Kathleen checked the office. The bookshelf stood against the wall, but it was much bigger than she'd anticipated and made the room smell of fresh wood and honey. But no Noah. Why should he be here? He had better things to do, no doubt. Even so, disappointment settled inside her.

She went to the other bedroom, hoping her exam table might be there, and couldn't believe her eyes. Her completed table sat against one wall, but it was so different than what she'd seen two days ago. Rather than plain wood, the top surface had burgundy vinyl padding attached with furniture tacks. A small dresser sat on the other side of the room, for supplies, with a rolling wooden stool next to it.

She couldn't believe he'd done all this.

The beeps of telephone buttons being pressed drew Kathleen's attention. She went to her office doorway. What was Jessica up to?

Jessica's voice held a chipper tone. "Hello, Hannah? This is Jessica Yoder."

Kathleen listened to the back-and-forth chatter for a minute, then went back into her office. If this was why Jessica wanted to come—to use the phone freely so their parents wouldn't overhear—Kathleen would need to put a stop to that. She would broach the subject when they stopped for lunch. For now, she'd let her sister enjoy a little freedom.

Kathleen spent the morning organizing her medical supplies and figuring out a filing system. She created forms by hand she would need when charting people's health concerns and made a list of office supplies for preparing and labeling patients' medical records.

A bit before noon, she exited her office and found Jessica sitting on the kitchen table with her legs swinging, still on the phone. The girl must have made twenty calls by now. Hanging up from one and immediately dialing another. Should Kathleen leave this for *Dat* and *Mum* to deal with? *Ne*. Jessica had come with her, and in so doing, she'd allowed her baby sister to over-use the phone. It was her fault.

Jessica said goodbye, took the phone from her ear and turned it off.

"Jessica."

Her sister held up her hand. "Just a sec." She picked up a spiral notebook, jotted something down, set it aside and then hopped down from the table. "Sorry. I meant to get lunch set out, but time got away from me." She lifted the cloth off the top of the basket. "Is Noah joining us?"

Since Kathleen hadn't seen Noah all morning, she guessed not. "I doubt it. I need to talk to you about what you've done with your time all morning."

Jessica's face brightened, and she retrieved the notebook, turning it to face Kathleen. "You have three appointments this afternoon."

Kathleen stared at the lined page. Hannah Zook at one thirty. Martha Beiler at two. And Grace Troyer at two thirty. She looked from the page to Jessica several times. "How…? How did you…?" Finally, she settled on, "How?"

Jessica patted the community phone book lying on the table. "I just kept calling people. Most turned me down politely. A few sputtered and hung up, claiming they had something urgent that needed attending to. We both know, we Amish aren't the urgent type."

"I can't believe you called all those people and scrounged up appointments for me."

"Well, if we're going to have telephones, we might as well put them to *gut* use. There were a lot of people I couldn't get a hold of because they don't have telephones in their homes, only shared ones out at the street."

Kathleen hugged Jessica. *"Danki."* Her clinic was actually getting started. Her dream realized. Finally. Everything was coming together. "And here I thought… Oh, never mind."

"You thought I was calling my friends."

Kathleen nodded.

Jessica averted her gaze and pulled her mouth sideways. "I confess. I did call a couple of my friends and quickly told them what I was doing and then asked them if anyone in their house needed to see the doctor."

Kathleen smiled. "As far as I'm concerned, talking to your friends needed to be done in order to get around to the question of a doctor visit. You can't jump right in asking if they need an appointment. I overheard your first call where you were doing just that."

Jessica jumped off the table. "Shall we eat?"

"*Ja.* Would you set everything out? I'll go find Noah. After all, *Mum* did pack that lunch for him too."

"All right." Jessica turned to the basket.

Kathleen would check the barn first and then the house. She opened the door to the *dawdy haus* and hurried out before her sister could change her mind. In her haste to close the door, she wasn't paying attention to where she was going and literally ran into the object of her search and tottered off balance.

Noah grabbed her upper arms and kept her upright.

Kathleen gazed into his brown eyes that appeared as startled as she was. Then she noticed his neck flush. Then she remembered the mattress incident two days ago—the last time she'd seen him—and how long he'd stared at her then. Was he also thinking of the incident that had thrown them so close together?

He didn't say anything. Just stared. As she was doing as well.

The door latch clicked behind her, and she sensed it swing open.

Jessica.

Noah jerked his hands away from Kathleen's arms as though she burned him. He straightened and cleared his throat. "Jessica. I didn't know you would be here today."

Jessica spoke. "Here I am. *Gut*. She found you already. I was just setting out lunch. When *Mum* said there would be enough for all three of us, she must have meant for five."

Everyone laughed. Amish women tended to prepare far more food than the number of people could eat. There seemed to be an unspoken motto that no one should go hungry or even think they might go hungry.

Kathleen's three afternoon appointments turned out to be social visits. Ladies she knew from the community who wanted to catch up.

She was disappointed, to be sure. But it was a start.

Two days later, Noah drove to the Yoders' for Sunday singing, Bible study and fellowship. On the Sundays between regular community church services, they always included him, whether at their house or at their son-in-law and daughter's, Titus and Gloria Schrock. Noah was grateful for their generosity and thoughtfulness. He loathed staying home alone when he knew the rest of the community would be getting together in small and large groups to fellowship with each other.

He often rode on horseback to the Yoders', but today, he drove the two-wheeled trap as the day was sunny and he brought a box of food. He was in no way lacking in provisions. He still had jars of food given to him for six months after Rachel died. The older women wanted to make sure he had enough to eat during his grief, and the young women wanted to show off their homemaking abilities to a potential husband.

The inpouring of generosity had been humbling. He still received occasional jars of food, loaves of bread, muffins, pies and cakes. Because he had plenty to eat, he wanted to contribute to the meals. So he'd brought some hard-boiled eggs, biscuits and a stew he'd made out of jars of canned goods. Green beans, corn, potatoes, tomatoes and beef. Not as *gut* as Rachel's or Pamela's, but edible. They obviously did something more than just pour the contents of jars into a pot and heat them.

He settled in the parlor with the Yoder family, which felt like his own. One of the many blessings of being Amish was one never need be alone if one didn't want to be. Simply drive to a neighbor's to visit. Amish always had time. Kathleen smiled at him, and something inside him shifted slightly. He wasn't sure what it was. Probably just indigestion. But he hadn't eaten anything. So he ignored the feeling and pulled his harmonica from his pants pocket.

Kathleen tilted her head. "You play?"

He nodded. "It keeps me from singing. I'm not so *gut*."

"I'm sure you sing as well as any of us."

He didn't. He hurt his own ears when he tried, which he hadn't done in over two decades. His *vater* had given him the harmonica to help him save face. Everyone was required to "make a joyful noise unto the Lord" unless they played one of the three instruments that were allowed. Harmonica, guitar and accordion. Harmonica being the only one to excuse him from using his voice. But even *Gott* had to be relieved when Noah started playing instead of singing.

After the miniservice and meal, they divvied up into their usual teams for softball. David, Benjamin, Joshua, Jessica and ten-year-old Nancy on one team, and Titus, Noah, Samuel, Ruby and six-year-old Andrew on the other. Pamela sat on the sidelines with the two younger children, Mark and Luke, on a quilt. Kathleen didn't have a place in any of the groups, so she sat with her *mutter* and older sister.

Noah crossed to her. "You can be on our team."

"You already have even teams."

"That's all right. There's always room for one more. Besides, Andrew usually tires out and wanders off. He comes back when it's his turn to bat. You'll even up the sides." He held out a worn baseball glove. "I hear you used to be *gut*."

A smile broke across her face. "I don't know about that, though I could hold my own. But I haven't played in years. I probably won't be any *gut* now."

"That's all right."

She took the glove and stood. "What position do you want me at?"

He smiled back at her. "I hear you were a decent pitcher."

She had played on college intramural teams and on the resident doctors' team. No one had expected much from the little Amish girl, but she'd surprised a few people.

She joined the other players. When it was six-year-old Andrew's turn to bat, the boy asked for Noah's help. Noah stood behind him and gripped the bat with him. On the fifth swing, the bat connected with the ball. No one was counting strikes for him.

Noah hoisted Andrew up and ran for first base. "Drop the bat. Drop the bat."

Andrew did, finally, release the bat once the pair stopped at first base. Safe.

That had been very sweet of Noah to help Kathleen's nephew. She couldn't imagine her fellow doctors doing that. They were far too competitive. But for her Amish people, this was about family and building relationships and having a *gut* time.

Kathleen hadn't had this much fun in a long time. With the other medical residents and interns, the pressure not to make even the smallest mistake and to win had been fierce, as though someone's life depended on them winning. It was the reason she'd quit playing with them long ago.

She was glad Noah had talked her into it. He had a *gut* heart and seemed to understand what she needed.

On Monday, Kathleen walked to Noah's alone. Jessica had gone with their *mum* to Gloria's to help her for the morning. The dark clouds overhead threatened rain. As she strolled into the yard, Noah led his horse and larger, covered buggy out of the barn. She crossed to him. "Are you going into town?"

He seemed startled at her presence and hesitant to answer. *"Ja."*

"Could I tag along? I need to get a few office supplies, file folders and such." She smiled brightly in the hopes of coaxing one out of him.

He remained straight-faced. "Sure." He helped her in and drove off down the road.

Silence weighed heavy in the confined space. Something was troubling him today. He seemed to want to be alone.

"Noah, would you pull over?"

He turned his head and focused his gaze on her. "What? Why?"

"I'll walk back. It's not more than a half a mile."

"I thought you wanted to go into town."

"I did. I do. But I can go another day." The office supplies could wait. It wasn't as though she had a slew of patients to keep track of.

"It could start raining any moment."

"I don't mind the rain."

But he kept driving. "What changed your mind about going into town?"

She hadn't wanted to mention anything, just to allow him to keep his private thoughts to himself. But now she had no choice. "You didn't seem eager for me to come along." That sounded petty. "I don't mean you should be overjoyed with my presence. I just mean that you seem deep in thought and would probably like to be alone, and I've intruded on that."

"*Ne.* I mean *ja.* I do have a lot of thoughts, but you're not intruding. I want you along."

"Are you sure?"

"*Ja.*"

"All right."

He shifted on the seat. "I'm going into town to look for someone."

"Please don't feel as though you have to explain yourself to me or make conversation. I'm content to just be here." *Beside you and enjoying your presence.*

He remained quiet for some time before he spoke again. "My *mutter.*"

"Your *mutter*? What about her?"

"I'm going to look for her."

"She's in town?"

He nodded. "I've seen her."

"This is none of my business and you don't have to tell me anything, but you've *seen* her? You said you were going to *look* for her. Why is she in town and not with your *vater*?"

"She left us when I was a teenager and we lived on the other side of the county. After my *vater* and I moved into this community, I never expected to see her again. But I've seen her in town many times over the years. I saw her the other time we came into town together. But I don't know where she lives nor have I ever talked to her."

Kathleen didn't know what to say. She had so many questions, but none of this was her business. He could tell her more if he wanted to.

"I don't know why she left us. And I don't know why she's moved to this town. She still dresses Amish."

"I hope you find her. This is a very personal trip for you, so if need be, I can walk back alone, as I said."

"*Ne.* I want you along. I don't know what to say to her. I don't know how to find her. I don't know if I even want to find her."

"I will go with you." She felt honored he would share so much with her. "Tell me what you would like me to do."

"I don't know. I need to find out where she lives."

"If we locate a city phone book, we can see if she's listed. If she has a phone, she should be in there."

"Why would she have a phone?"

Kathleen tipped her head. "Possibly for a similar reason she's living in town?"

Once in town, they used a phone book at a local business and found an address for a woman who could be his *mutter.* When they got there and knocked, his *mutter* wasn't home. Or if she was, she didn't come to the door.

Noah took up the reins. "It's best this way.

Gott's will." He drove out of town without remembering that Kathleen had wanted to pick up a few things.

That was fine. This trip had never been about her. She ached for Noah's loss.

Chapter Eight

Noah stood high on a roof gable truss at the barn raising of the bishop's eldest grandson. His *vater* held a board in place while Noah tapped a nail until it held on its own. Then, making sure his elbow was steady, he took a hard swing and sank the rest of the nail in one blow. He'd practiced many hours when he was young to be consistent in his aim. Some of the younger men and boys tried to copy Noah, but none were quite as successful.

Yet all he received from his *vater* was a slight smirk on one side of his mouth and a shake of his head.

Noah pointed with his hammer as he retrieved another nail from the canvas pouch tied around his waist. "Not like when I was a lad."

"You've come a long way, but this isn't a show."

Noah lined up the next nail and got it to hold in place as he did the other one. "I know."

"Do you?"

Why couldn't his *vater* appreciate Noah's work? "It saves time and energy. Why swing the hammer multiple times when you can get the job done with one?"

"You're quite proud of this ability, aren't you?"

"Ja." Why shouldn't he be?

"If you were truly doing it to save time and energy, then it would be something worthy. But you do it to show off. 'Pride goeth before a fall.'"

"I just want you to be…"

"Proud of you?"

Noah bristled. *"Ja."*

His *vater* wasn't nearly as hard on him as he used to be, but his rebuff still stung.

"I'm pleased when you act as a *gut* Amish should. And a *gut* Amish would not be seeking approval from men but from *Gott*. Honor *Gott*, and I'll be pleased enough."

Though it couldn't hurt to get a little approval now and then, his *vater* was right. The only approval that truly mattered was from *Gott*. But still…

He glanced to the yard below to catch a

glimpse of Kathleen among the women setting out the noon meal.

As though she knew he was seeking her out, her gaze turned up to the skeleton of the barn, and she smiled at him. It warmed him all over. *She* appreciated his carpentry skills.

Soon, the call sounded for the lunch break.

Noah scrambled down with all the other men on the upper part of the barn.

As he stood in line with his *vater*, waiting to fill a plate with food, he could still feel the tension of his earlier foolishness of wanting his *vater*'s approval. The only way to shake it from his thoughts was to broach an equally tense subject. "I saw her in town."

His *vater* stiffened and turned. "Your *mutter*?"

"Ja."

His *vater*'s eyes widened. "Are you sure it was her?"

"Ja." He wouldn't complicate things by telling him he'd seen her more than once and over several years.

After a moment, his *vater* spoke softly. "What did you say to her?"

"Nothing. There wasn't time. Besides, I wouldn't know what to say"

"Ask her the question you kept asking me."

"It doesn't matter anymore why she left. She

left us, and she's gone. She could have come home if she'd wanted to." But Noah did still want to know the answer.

Had it been something he'd done? Could he have said or done something to make her stay? A mistake he feared repeating.

Was that the real reason he shied away from marrying again? Not so much fear that a wife would leave him by one means or another, but that her leaving would be his fault.

Kathleen hadn't realized how enjoyable a barn raising could be. The smell of the wood mingled with that of the food. The sounds of children playing, people talking and hammers striking nails mingled together in a beautiful symphony. Women bustled around with the food. Children scampered about. Men constructed and climbed on the ever-growing structure.

She'd missed these kinds of community gatherings while away. *Englishers* gathered, of course, but not as a whole community and not to help someone else. Their get-togethers were more self-serving and usually only for enjoyment. A party for this thing or that, or for nothing at all. They never seemed to lack for a reason to throw a party.

After six weeks back, she'd had only ten patient visits. And half of those were her own family. Likely because they took pity on her. Jessica had been mostly unsuccessful at drumming up patients willing to come in. Preacher Hochstetler must be discouraging them. He'd certainly made the evils of higher education clear in his sermon this past Sunday.

Lord, how can I make him see the gut in having a doctor close by? Even a female Amish doctor.

Ne. It wasn't hers to persuade him or anyone else. That was *Gott*'s responsibility. He was the heart changer.

Don't let our community suffer because of stubbornness or pride.

While away on *Rumspringa*, Kathleen had felt out of place in the English world. And when she first returned, she'd felt the same way in her Amish community. But each week, she found herself more and more at home here. She wanted *gut* things for her people, and the clinic *would* be *gut* for them. No question about that.

She stood at the end of the food line, placing a roll on each man's plate.

Noah stopped in front of her. *"Guten Nachmittag."*

"Guten Nachmittag." She placed a roll on his plate. "You men are doing a fine job."

"Danki. Kathleen, this is my *vater*, Abraham."

"Nice to meet you."

Abraham thinned his lips. "So you're the doctor. Have any patients yet?"

She wished her Amish neighbors weren't so slow to accept her. "A few. You should come by."

"Maybe I will. It's on my son's farm, you know."

Well, that was more open than some people. Many either wouldn't acknowledge her as a doctor or just didn't even talk to her because they didn't know what to say. Oh, they would smile but then hurry away as though she were contagious.

Noah studied his *vater* with an expression of longing as though he wanted something. Something more. But what? She sensed approval?

A high-pitched scream cut through the air. A scream of pain.

Kathleen whirled around. As fast as she was, her sister Gloria was faster. She was in the midst of three of her children—Nancy, Andrew and Mark—faster than a city taxi driver vying for a fare.

Four-year-old Mark waved his pudgy little hand back and forth. Tears stained his round cheeks and continued to flow while he wailed.

Gloria tried to still her son's hand. Though she had hold of his wrist, he still jerked his hand too much to see what was the matter. Gloria turned to her daughter. "What happened?"

By now, the men had gathered as well.

Nancy planted her hands on her slender hips. "Andrew dared him to pick up a bee."

"Andrew!" Gloria scolded her six-year-old son.

"I didn't think he'd do it. He did it wrong. He wouldn't got hurt if he'd cupped his hands around the clover to pick it up. Not put his hands around the bee."

"I don't care. You shouldn't have told him to do it in the first place. You're supposed to be looking out for him. Go sit on the porch until your *vater* decides what your punishment will be."

Andrew shuffled off.

Kathleen took hold of her nephew's hand. "We need to see if there's a stinger."

Gloria helped pry the four-year-old's hand open. The stinger sat in the middle finger of his shaking left hand.

"I can get that out for you." Kathleen carefully scraped her fingernail across Mark's skin. The stinger dislodged, and she flicked it away. "All gone."

Gloria rubbed her son's arm. "There now, you'll be fine."

But Mark didn't look fine and took a gasping breath.

Kathleen too gasped for breath. *Ne.* This wasn't happening. Not again. He wasn't having an allergic reaction. She was imagining it. Her mind playing a trick on her.

Gloria gazed at her with horror in her eyes. "Do something."

Her sister had seen it too. Kathleen jumped to her feet, dashed for her parents' buggy, retrieved her pack of medical supplies and ran back, out of breath. She had an epinephrine injector. She dug in her pack and quickly had the lifesaving medicine in hand. She knelt beside her sister and nephew.

"*Halt!* You can't do that without his *vater*'s permission," a male voice called from the crowd.

Kathleen glanced around.

Preacher Hochstetler.

Kathleen turned back to her sister.

Gloria lifted her chin and looked as though she was about to nod when Titus spoke up.

"What's going on?" He knelt on the other side of his son from Kathleen, next to his wife.

Preacher Hochstetler spoke. "She's trying to give your son something without your permission. She's not allowed to do that."

Kathleen bristled. "It's epinephrine. It will stop the allergic reaction from closing his throat so he can breathe better." She aimed the device for the boy's small leg.

"Don't!" Preacher Hochstetler barked, then spoke to Titus. "Don't let her do it."

Again Titus asked, "What happened?"

Through short breaths, Kathleen said, "Mark's been stung by a bee and is having an allergic reaction. If he doesn't get this medicine immediately, he could die. He's going into anaphylactic shock." Dare she go against Titus and the church leaders? If she did, she wouldn't be allowed to treat another person in their community. She couldn't stand by and watch her nephew die. She would deal with the consequences later.

She leaned forward on her knees.

Preacher Hochstetler held up his hand, and two men grabbed Kathleen's arms and pulled her to her feet.

"Don't believe her. Our children get stung all the time and don't need to be interfered with and poked with who knows what."

Titus's panicked gaze darted between Kathleen, his son, Gloria and the preacher.

Poor Titus. He was getting too much information all at once. And the pressure from Preacher Hochstetler was great. Titus seemed to want to allow Kathleen to treat his son. He also didn't want to go against one of the church leaders. He couldn't seem to get himself to take action.

Kathleen held out the lifesaving instrument to him. "Hold it firmly against his thigh and press the button."

Gloria spoke in a panicky voice. "Please, Titus. He's going to die. Our son is going to *die*."

Titus chewed his lower lip, obviously unsure what to do. So much peer pressure and tradition to overcome.

Noah said, "The leadership approved a trial period of her being a doctor for the district. You can let her treat him."

Kathleen continued to hold the epinephrine out. "Please take it. You can do it. It's easy. Hold it against his thigh and press the button."

Titus stared hard at the medicine as though he wanted to take it.

Gloria pleaded. "Please, Titus." Tears rolled down her cheeks. "Please."

Nancy snatched the allergy pen from Kathleen, jammed it into her brother's thigh and pressed the button before anyone protested.

Ja! Kathleen released her captive breath. Bless Nancy's heart for taking action. No one would be upset with her because she was a child.

Kathleen prayed that it hadn't been too late and Mark would recover. The men let go of her, and she watched the boy closely from the distance she was allowed to be, close but not touching him.

Though her nephew lay limp in his *mutter*'s arms, his breathing came a little easier.

And so did Kathleen's. "You should take him into town to a doctor. Don't let him scratch his hand. And he might have stomach pain and could vomit."

Titus carried his young son to their buggy.

Gloria turned to *Mum*. "Can you...?"

Mum handed baby Luke to Gloria. "Don't worry. We'll look after Nancy and Andrew."

Gloria squeezed her daughter's shoulder and mouthed, *"Danki."* Then she hustled to the buggy.

Kathleen crouched in front of Nancy. "You did the right thing. I'm very proud of you."

Andrew, who had returned from the porch, sobbed softly.

Kathleen hooked her arm around him. "Your brother is going to be all right."

"I never knowed the bee could do that to him. I've been stung before. He's been stung before too."

"When someone is allergic, each time they are stung the reaction can get worse." Kathleen pulled back and held him by his shoulders. "Do you understand that it's not your fault?"

Nodding, he sniffled and dragged his shirt-sleeve across his nose.

Everyone drifted off to eat.

Mum put a hand on Kathleen's shoulder. "Are you all right?"

Kathleen nodded. "I'm fine." Of course she was. However, as *Mum* walked away with Andrew and Nancy, promising them each a cookie, Kathleen thought how close her nephew had come to dying. Had relived her own sister dying. Her hands shook, and her breathing became labored again.

Heat flushed through her body, and she ground her teeth together. Preacher Hochstetler nearly cost Mark his life.

Her *mutter* called to her. "Kathleen, are you coming?"

Kathleen forced a cheery tone to her voice. "I'll be there in a minute." She hurried away and around the side of the house opposite where the men were building the barn and the food was set out. This had been too much like what had happened to Nancy eighteen years ago. She needed to be away from people to pull herself together. If anyone saw her hands shaking, they would never trust her to treat them.

She leaned against a large sugar maple tree, bent at the waist and rested her hands on her thighs. *Breathe in and out.* She obeyed her inner doctor voice. *Don't think about what could have happened. In and out. Don't think about what* did *happen all those years ago. Mark will be fine.*

"Kathleen?" Noah said.

She jerked upright with a small squeal. "Oh. I didn't… I wasn't expecting…"

"Are you all right?"

She pinched her bottom lip hard between her teeth and nodded. She *would* be all right if she could just erase the image of Mark struggling for breath.

"Mark was breathing easier by the time we got him to the buggy. I think he'll be fine."

"I saw my sister lying there in Mark's place. I saw her dying all over again." Tears she had been holding at bay cascaded over the lower rims of her eyes. "If my own brother-in-law won't let me treat his family, what hope do I have that anyone else will? None. I may as well quit right now. Why would *Gott* have me go through all that struggling and hardship for nothing? It doesn't make any sense."

"*Gott*'s ways are different than ours. Isaiah fifty-five, -eight and -nine say, 'For my thoughts are not your thoughts, neither are your ways my ways, saith the Lord. For as the heavens are higher than the earth, so are my ways higher than your ways.' Trust *Gott* to know what He's doing."

She thought she'd been doing that, but this made no sense. If she'd gone to all that trouble to go to med school and now wouldn't be allowed to help anyone, what was the use of it all?

Noah couldn't bear the anguish on Kathleen's face, so he glanced around. What he was about to do went against so many *Ordnung* rules, and he could be shunned. No one was in sight. He stepped forward and wrapped his arms around her. "It's all right." She needed comforting, and he wanted to comfort her.

She leaned into him and sobbed.

After a few minutes, when her crying softened, he pulled back. "You saved Mark's life."

Tears smeared her cheeks. She shook her head. "Nancy saved his life. I was helpless."

"If not for your medicine on hand, he would have died, so you both saved him." He cupped her face and brushed away her tears with his thumbs. Then, before he realized what he was doing, he pressed his lips to hers. He could *really* be shunned for this.

But she didn't resist. Quite the opposite. She kissed him back. *Definitely shunned.*

He pulled away and released her. "I'm sorry."

She didn't say anything, just stared up at him with her piercing blue eyes.

Though he wanted to stay here with her indefinitely, he knew they couldn't. "We should get back to the gathering."

She nodded.

He wanted to kiss her again, but instead, he turned and pushed the kiss out of his mind.

Chapter Nine

On Monday, Kathleen took her parents' buggy into town by herself. A town doctor had seen her nephew, declared him fit to go home the same day and prescribed an allergy pen so they would always have one on hand. And Titus had apologized to her for hesitating.

She pulled up in front of Noah's *mutter*'s house. As she walked up to the gate, the neighbor lady watering her flowers said, "Heddy's not there."

Kathleen turned. "Excuse me?"

"Heddy, the Amish woman who lives there. She's at work. You'll find her at the library."

"*Danki*—I mean, thank you." This was *gut*. She could tell Noah where his *mutter* worked.

However, to make sure, Kathleen drove to the library and spied a woman dressed in Amish garb in a row of shelves, returning books to their places. Must be Heddy Lambright. Kathleen pretended to be interested in titles nearby. So many questions she'd like to ask this woman. Why had she, who still dressed as an Amish, left her family and community? Why didn't she come back? Why didn't she talk to her son?

When Heddy finished and settled herself behind the checkout desk, Kathleen sauntered up. "I would like to apply for a library card, please."

Heddy stared at her a moment, then turned to the computer screen. "I know you don't have the kind of identification we normally request from patrons, like a driver's license or ID card, but do you have something with your address on it with you?"

Kathleen shook her head.

"I can issue you a library card, but what you can check out will be limited to three items. When you can bring in proof of address, we can lift that limitation." She put her hands on the computer keyboard. "Your full name and address."

Kathleen gave her the information.

Noah's *mutter* retrieved a card from a drawer and scanned in its preprinted bar code number. Then she handed it to Kathleen.

"Danki."

She spoke in a kindly tone. "I've been wondering what your name was."

Kathleen did a double take. "Excuse me?"

"I've seen you in town with my son, Noah. Are you his wife?"

This woman had seen her before? *"Ne."*

Heddy stiffened. "I thought you looked different than her. What are you doing with my son? Where's his wife?"

"She passed away."

Noah's *mutter* took a quick breath. "Oh. I'm sorry to hear that. I didn't know. How long ago?"

"Three years."

"You're why he shaved off his beard. I almost didn't recognize him."

He hadn't shaved it for Kathleen. It had been time. He'd said so. "Noah and I are just friends."

"He looks at you as more than a friend."

Did he? That made her smile inside, but she schooled her expression to not reveal her pleasure to the other woman.

Heddy gave a knowing smile. But just what did she know? "I imagine you have a lot of questions for me."

"They aren't mine to ask."

"Do you think my son will come to visit me?"

Kathleen didn't know if she should tell Heddy that Noah *had* tried, but the woman hadn't been home. That too was Noah's to do or not. It might break the woman's heart to know she missed an opportunity to talk with her son. "I can't say. But he does know that you live in town."

"*Ja*, I've seen him see me."

Kathleen ached for this woman. "Have you thought about going and talking to him?"

"I'm shunned for leaving my husband. I have no right to go to him. He's not allowed to talk to me. You could be shunned for interacting with me."

"I'm not a member yet."

"Why not?" Heddy frowned. "I'm sorry. I have no right to ask."

"I'm going through the classes and will become a member in the fall, but I did something unorthodox. I stayed away for fourteen years, attended college and became a doctor. Now I'm trying to get the community to accept me as *their* physician."

Noah's *mutter* chuckled. "That's not going to be easy. The men in leadership are generally rigid in their ways."

"*Ja*, some of them are. But your son is part of the leadership."

"He is?"

"*Ja*, and he's allowed me to set up my clinic in his *dawdy haus*."

"I'm glad to hear my son is open to new ideas. Not everything new or different is bad."

Kathleen liked this woman.

"Would you tell my Noah that I always set a place for him at my table?"

Heddy's way of saying she'd like a visit from her son warmed Kathleen's heart.

"I feel I've already intruded where maybe I shouldn't have."

The woman dipped her head slightly. "I understand."

When Kathleen left, she yearned to stay and talk with Heddy longer. She felt a kindred spirit with this woman who lived in the *Englisher* world but remained Amish and separated from her people and her son as Kathleen had done when she went to med school.

That Wednesday, Noah headed next door while Kathleen was in her new clinic. He had to talk to David. He'd prayed and tried to talk himself out of needing to make this visit, but he saw no way around it.

As he walked on the edge of the blacktop, Kathleen's *vater* slowed his buggy alongside Noah. "Can we give you a lift?" He and Pamela were coming from the direction of town.

"I was on my way over to see you. I have a matter I wish to speak with you about." Noah stood beside the buggy.

Pamela turned her focus on him. "You'll come for supper. Would you like to talk then?"

"That would be *gut*." Then he could get back before Kathleen noticed his absence. "I'll drive Kathleen over in time to help with supper preparations." He jogged back toward his house, and the buggy continued down the road.

Before Kathleen finished in her clinic, Noah returned and hitched up the trap. He led the horse out of the barn, up to the *dawdy haus* and looped the reins around the porch rail. He walked inside.

Kathleen sat prim and proper on the sofa with her hands folded in her lap.

He raised an eyebrow. "What are you doing?"

"Seeing what it will be like for my patients to sit here and wait. That is if I ever have any more."

"Aren't your sister and Titus having you oversee Mark after his reaction to the bee sting?"

"*Ja*, but fortunately there's not much for me to do. They're going to the allergy specialist to get Mark desensitized to bee venom."

"But they'll likely come to you for other things now that they know you saved their son's life."

She smiled. "*Danki*. I was feeling sorry for myself, and you just cheered me up."

Not his intention, but he had wanted her to feel better. *"Bitte."* And she was quite pretty when she smiled. "I've hitched up the trap."

She stood and crossed the room. "You don't have to take me home. I can walk."

"Your *mutter* invited me to supper."

She tilted her head in a very cute way. "She did? When?"

"They were passing by on the road. I said *hallo* to them. Are you ready?"

She grabbed her pack of medical supplies and preceded him out the door. She locked it with the key he'd given her.

Once in the buggy, Kathleen fidgeted in the seat next to him.

"Is something the matter?" He was already nervous enough without her twitchiness.

She picked at the folds in her apron. "I've done something you might not be pleased with."

He couldn't imagine what that could be. "It's generally best just to say it quickly."

"I went into town the other day."

He frowned. "Have I given you the impression you need my permission to do things or go places?"

"*Ne.* It's what I *did* in town."

"You have me quite curious. The ride to your house isn't long, so if you're going to tell me, you might want to do so soon."

She took a deep breath. "I—I spoke to your *mutter.*"

His breath froze in his lungs. He wished

they had already arrived. He wished he hadn't pressed her to tell him. He wished he hadn't asked if something was the matter.

"Please say something. Are you angry with me?"

"I don't know."

"Your *mutter* seems very nice and is interested in you and your life."

"She is?"

"*Ja.* She's said she's sorry for the loss of your wife. And…"

"And what?"

"She sets a place for you at her table. She asked me to tell you that."

So his *mutter* welcomed a visit from him. Was he ready to actually talk to her? He didn't know.

"She works at the library. You can find her there if she's not at home."

Did he *want* to find her? A part of him did and another part didn't. Reconciliation warred with punishment. She was the one who had left and stayed away. He turned into the Yoders' driveway.

"Noah?"

He faced Kathleen. "I don't know just how I feel about you speaking to my *mutter*, but I know I'm not angry."

"*Danki.*"

The tight hold he kept on the unknown loosened inside him, freeing him to wonder what talking to his *mutter* would be like. She set a place for him? So why not return?

Once at a stop, Noah parted ways from Kathleen to unhitch his horse and find her *vater*. He needed to put thoughts of his *mutter* aside for now.

David Yoder sat in the cool of the barn, running a file across an ax blade. He looked up and, seeing Noah, stopped. "Is it that time already?" He rubbed his thumb across the blade, then set the ax aside.

"There's still time." Noah had been sure of himself earlier, but now he wasn't so sure.

Kathleen's *vater* gave Noah his full attention. "You wanted to speak to me?"

He couldn't back down now. He had no choice. After what he'd done, this was the only reasonable action. "I would like your permission to court Kathleen."

A wide smile broke across David's face. "You had me scared for a second. I thought you were going to tell me something terrible. Of course you can court her. I already think of you as a son. I'd be proud to have it official."

If David knew what Noah had done, he might not be so eager. But Noah was fixing his transgression. No need to incriminate Kathleen. He was to blame.

When they went inside, David whispered in Pamela's ear before seating himself at the table. Pamela beamed at Noah. David had obviously told her.

After supper, Noah asked Kathleen to go for a walk with him.

"I can't. I have supper dishes to help with."

Pamela waved her hand toward Kathleen. "You go. Jessica and I will clean up the dishes."

"What?" Jessica said. "It's not my turn."

"Hush now," Pamela chided.

Jessica huffed over to the sink.

Kathleen called after her, "I'll do them the next two times it's your turn."

That made Jessica smile.

As Noah walked Kathleen out to the large black walnut tree with the swing hanging from it, she spoke. "Is this about talking to your *mutter*?"

"Ne." He was actually relieved she'd done that. The ice had been broken. "I told you I wasn't angry at you for that. I'll need to decide what to do, though."

She stared at him a moment as though trying to decide what to say, but instead she sat on the swing and remained quiet for another moment. *"Danki* for reminding me that people will likely start seeking me out for their medical needs. But none so far."

He appreciated the change in subject. She was *gut* at relieving tension that way. "It's true. I heard several men at the barn raising talking about Mark and what you did."

"Did they sound like they would allow their wives and children to come to my clinic?"

They hadn't said anything close to that. They just talked about the incident. "I don't think it will be long before your waiting room is full." At least he hoped that was the case. He walked around behind her. "Here, let me push you."

She gripped the ropes, and he pulled the swing back, then pushed her forward. He pushed her higher and higher.

After a bit, she dragged her feet on the ground and brought herself to a stop. "That was fun. I haven't swung since I was a girl. But I do feel guilty about the work I left to *Mum* and my sisters. I should go inside."

Before she could stand, Noah came around in front of her. "Wait. I have something to ask you first."

She tilted her head back to gaze up at him. So pretty in the waning sunlight.

He couldn't put this off any longer. "I already spoke to your *vater*."

She cocked her head to one side. "About what?"

"Courting you. And he gave his permission."

Her sweet expression turned to confusion. "You what? Why would you do that?"

"Don't tell me you didn't expect this?" And he only asked to court her because he'd crossed a line he shouldn't have. Nothing more. If he hadn't kissed her, he wouldn't even be considering this. Would he?

"Why in the world would I expect this? Is it because you're letting me use your *dawdy haus*? You think I owe you or something?"

"*Ne*. This has nothing to do with the *dawdy haus*. It has to do with me kissing you at the barn raising. I had no right to do that. Now I'm trying to make that right."

"By *courting* me? It was just a kiss. It didn't mean anything."

That was the *Englisher* influence in her talking.

"You didn't tell *Dat* we kissed, did you?"

He shook his head. "Of course not. But he was quite pleased for us to court."

With her feet, she pushed the swing back away from him until she stood with the seat at her back. "You had no right to ask him." She untangled herself from the ropes.

"But he already gave his permission. What will I tell him?"

"I don't know. Don't you understand? I can't court you."

"Why not? Is there someone else?" The thought of someone else courting her twisted his insides.

"I can't court anyone because I'm never going to get married."

"Never? Why not? You're still young."

"Because *Gott* called me to be a doctor. If I marry, I won't be able to be a doctor. It's a sacrifice I made a long time ago. Having the medicine to save my nephew is proof to me that *Gott does* want me to be a doctor."

"Kathleen, we kissed. We *really* kissed. I'm just trying to do the right thing by you."

"The *right thing* is to pretend it never happened. I need to go inside now." She scooted past him.

That moment was seared into his brain. He caught her arm. "But I can't pretend I never kissed you."

"You have to."

Now he wanted to be upset with her for talking to his *mutter*. He needed something to pin his anger on. But his *mutter* had nothing to do with this madness.

He let Kathleen slip from his grasp.

Kathleen ran into the house. She fancied Noah. More than she should. She had to keep herself from accepting his offer. Every fiber of her being wanted to say *ja*. But she couldn't court Noah Lambright or anyone else. Courtship led to a marriage proposal. A proposal led to marriage. No Amish man would allow his wife to continue working as a doctor. Noah *had* supported her and seemed like the type of man who would let her still be a doctor. But when children came along, he would insist she quit. She'd gone through too much, been away from her family for too long, to have it all be for naught.

Tears filled her eyes.

As a young girl, she'd dreamed of marrying a *gut* Amish man exactly like Noah and having lots of children. But when Nancy died and Kathleen decided to become a doctor, not having a husband and family was the price for helping her community. Unlike the English women, she couldn't have it all. She'd had to choose. Wife and *mutter*—or doctor.

Kathleen entered the house as her family sat in the living room for the evening devotional. She hurried past them and ran upstairs. In the room she shared with her sisters, she went to the window and peered out.

Noah stared up at the house, his gaze locking on hers. For a long moment, she watched him watching her. Both knew they saw each other, but neither turned away.

Noah lifted a hand in farewell and trudged off to the barn.

"Why, Lord?" she whispered. "Why send a man like Noah Lambright into my life? A man I could fall in love with, if not for the calling You gave me. Why dangle that dream in front of me? Is this a test? A test to see how committed I am to You?"

A soft knock sounded on the door. "Kathleen? It's *Mum*."

She didn't want to talk to anyone right now. She needed to sort out her thoughts. But it would be rude to turn her *mum* away. "Come in."

The door creaked slightly, then *Mum* spoke. "Are you coming back down?"

Kathleen shook her head. "Not tonight." She needed time alone to figure things out. Time to think.

Mum joined her by the window. "What's wrong? Did you quarrel with Noah?"

"Not exactly."

Through the window, Kathleen saw Noah coming out of the barn, leading his horse and trap. He climbed aboard, and the dream of a different life drove away.

He didn't rush up the driveway as though he were angry. He didn't glance back to see if she was still watching. He left at the normal, leisurely Amish pace.

"What is it, dear?"

Kathleen continued to stare out the window until Noah was out of sight. "Noah asked to court me."

"I know. Your *dat* and I couldn't be happier. He's already like a son to us."

Kathleen faced her *mum*. "I told him *ne*."

Mum's smile slipped away. "What? Why? He's a *gut* man. He'll make you a *gut* husband and *vater* to your children."

Kathleen's vision blurred. "I can't marry him. I can't marry anyone. *Gott* called me to be a doctor." *Gott* had dangled her childhood dream of a husband and family right in front of her. To tempt her? To tease her? Why?

Why couldn't Noah pretend they'd never kissed? Why did he have to be so honorable? Why did he need to do the right thing?

Mum spoke with compassion in her voice. "Why did you come back home then? Why take the classes to join church?"

"*Gott* didn't call me to just be a doctor, but a doctor for our community. I want to join church because I'm Amish." She tapped her fingertips on her chest. "In here. I know I'm not technically Amish until I join church. All through school and my residency, I continued to dress and behave as though I were still part of our community. One of the things that got me through being away was that I would be coming home and becoming a true member of this community. If I don't join church now, I *could* be a doctor for this community. The church leaders said so, but it would break my heart to not be truly Amish."

"You don't care for Noah at all? You can't picture yourself married to him? You don't wish to marry?"

"As a girl I dreamed of marrying someone like Noah. He is a man I think I could fall in love with. But I can't be a doctor if I marry. No husband, not even Noah, would allow his wife to be a doctor. Then what was all my sacrifice for? I might as well have stayed here and been happy instead of out in the world lonely and struggling."

Mum nodded. "Now I begin to understand all you sacrificed." She wrapped her arms around Kathleen. "You gave up one part of the life you wanted for another." She pulled back. "I think he cares a great deal for you."

She wanted to say that he didn't, that he'd asked out of a sense of duty, but then she would need to explain why she thought that way. And she couldn't tell her *mum* that Noah had kissed her. She would then be pressured to marry him. That would make the church leaders happy. Marry Kathleen Yoder off, and then they wouldn't have to hear any more about her being a doctor. Noah was part of the leadership.

A terrible, eerie, spine-chilling thought crawled up her back. Had Noah been tasked with courting her and marrying her to keep her from being trouble in the community? To keep her under control? Under *their* control? To keep her from being a doctor? To make an example out of her to everyone else to prove that going to college would amount to nothing?

She didn't want to think Noah capable of such manipulation. He seemed genuine in his help. If his request to court her was just some ploy, why would he have offered her the use of his *dawdy haus*? A way to control her? He *was* a member of the church leadership, after all.

Kathleen leaned into her *mum*'s embrace. "What am I going to do?"

"Pray. Ask *Gott* for guidance. Follow *Gott* first, then your heart."

The next day, Kathleen arrived at Noah's *dawdy haus*, but he wasn't inside as he usually was. She wasn't sure what to do. She needed to talk to him. She needed to know if there was even any point to having the clinic. Was it all just a farce?

She went to the big house and knocked. No answer. She went to the barn. He wasn't there either. Out of options, she sat in one of the rocking chairs on his porch to wait.

Sometime later, she heard her name being called. She opened her eyes to see Noah looking down at her. "I'm sorry. I didn't mean to fall asleep." This old habit was going to be a stubborn one to break. But if she was going to fall asleep and wake up to someone's face, she liked it being his. She stood.

He scrubbed his hand across his clean-shaven face. "I wasn't sure you'd come after last night."

"I wasn't sure if I would either. But I thought it best if we talked about this rather than letting it fester under the surface. I need to ask you a question, and I need an honest answer no matter what it is."

"I have always been honest with you. I see no reason not to be."

He might when he heard her question.

"Did the church leadership put you up to asking to court me as a means to control me?"

His mouth dropped open. "Whatever would make you think that?"

"Some of the leadership members aren't pleased with my plans to be a doctor in the community. If I married, I wouldn't be able to be a doctor, and their problems are solved. So?"

"*Ne.* They had nothing to do with my asking to court you. I asked because I stepped over the line by kissing you. I never should have done that. It was wrong of me. But know this, I would never ask to court you or anyone else, because the leaders asked me to. And believe me, they have asked."

She was glad to hear that. "I appreciate your honesty."

"The only reason I asked was because I kissed you."

"The *only* reason?" Not because he might like her even just a little bit. Even though both their *mutters* seemed to think he did.

"The only reason. I promise you."

She hesitated a moment before broaching her next topic. "About my clinic being in your *dawdy haus*. Since I turned down your offer of courtship, I assume you'd like me to find someplace else."

He shook his head. "*Ne*. We have done too much work to get it set up here. By the time you found someplace else and moved everything, the summer would be almost over and you'd be out of time to prove to the leaders that you should be allowed to continue as a doctor."

She couldn't figure him out. He was a member of the church leaders, but he seemed to favor her practicing medicine. "Why are you supporting my clinic so much?"

He lowered his head and rubbed the back of

his neck before meeting her gaze. "I often wonder if Rachel and our baby could have been saved if there had been someone like you close at hand."

Her heart ached for him. But she dared not ask the cause of death. Would he want to know if a physician could have made a difference? Or was it better not to know? Kathleen had been haunted with the knowledge that her sister *would* have lived had there been a medical facility close. No amount of medical knowledge or medicines would save everyone, but many could be spared.

"I admire your dedication, perseverance and desire to become a doctor. What you have done is incredible. I couldn't have done it."

She drank in his praise. Coming from anyone else, it wouldn't mean as much.

He picked up a box she hadn't noticed from the porch floor. "I got a few more supplies for the clinic. File folders, pens, a desk lamp, coffee, tea and sugar for the kitchen."

"Did you buy all that?"

He didn't answer.

"You didn't have to buy supplies for my clinic. You have already done so much."

"I wanted to."

She felt indebted to him and really felt guilty for turning him down last night. But he'd asked only because he felt guilty. Guilt was no reason to begin a courtship. She'd been right to turn him down. "Will we be able to go on as though nothing has happened between us?"

He straightened. "Nothing *has* happened."

The words *the kiss* bubbled up in her throat, but she tamped them down.

Chapter Ten

Kathleen stood in the kitchen with *Mum* and Ruby. She and Ruby had been tasked with peeling the potatoes for supper.

Jessica had been sent out to the garden to pick other vegetables they would need. She rushed back inside with her basket full. Tomatoes, peas, carrots, onions, garlic, as well as rhubarb to make a pie. "Kathleen has company, *Mum*." Her face was beaming from ear to ear.

Kathleen couldn't imagine who would be visiting her. Certainly not anyone to cause Jessica to smile so wide. "Who?"

"I don't know. He's talking to *Dat*. But he drove up in a shiny red sports car."

Kathleen widened her eyes. A sports car? Who could it be? The only people she knew who drove cars were *Englishers*, and the only *Englishers* she knew who would drive a sports car were doctors. What doctor would be visiting her?

Mum said, "Are you expecting anyone?"

"*Ne.* Maybe he has the wrong place."

Jessica shook her head. "I heard him mention your name."

Ruby set down the potato she was peeling and dried her hands. "Kathleen has an admirer." She headed for the front room. "I want to see him."

An admirer? Not likely. Kathleen wiped her hands on a towel and followed Ruby. Jessica and *Mum* followed as well. Ruby drew back the curtain, and all four of them peered out the front window.

"Who is it?" Jessica asked.

"Do you know him?" Ruby asked.

Kathleen shifted into a better position to see. The large black walnut tree out front blocked her view of *Dat* and the man, so she moved to the other end of the window and pulled the curtain back there.

Dat and the man strolled toward the house.

When they came into view, the man looked familiar. Then he smiled.

Kathleen sucked in a breath, dropped the curtain and stepped back, all in one motion.

Ruby studied her. "I'd say Kathleen knows him."

"Who is he?" *Mum* asked.

Kathleen swallowed. "Ethan Parker. He was one of the doctors in the hospital I did my residency in."

"He's cute," Jessica said.

"Come away from the window." *Mum* shooed her hands toward them. "You don't want him to catch you all gawking. Back into the kitchen. All of you."

Jessica and Ruby dutifully obeyed.

Mum caught Kathleen's arm and slowed her down. "Who is this Dr. Parker?"

"Just a doctor."

"He's gone out of his way to see you."

"We don't know he came to see me."

Mum planted her hands on her hips and gave her a look.

"All right. He must have come to see me. But I don't know why. I certainly never expected him."

With the sound of footsteps on the porch, *Mum* quickly ushered Kathleen back into the kitchen. Then spoke to all three of them. "Hush now, girls. No talking about this man."

Ruby spoke up. "Then I'll talk about Jonathan. I'm very excited about getting married this fall."

Kathleen had met Jonathan a couple of times this summer but hadn't gotten to really know him. When he visited, he spent all his time with Ruby, gazing at her.

The front door opened and closed. Kathleen went still and quiet, and quit listening to Ruby talk about her almost fiancé. Engagements weren't announced until the official proposal came through the bishop in the fall.

Kathleen couldn't make out what *Dat* and Ethan were saying. She thought to motion for her sisters and *Mum* to be quiet and realized they weren't talking but listening as well.

Then *Dat's* voice grew closer.

Mum whispered, "Get back to work."

Everyone resumed their tasks.

Kathleen picked up the half-skinned potato and peeler as *Dat* walked into the kitchen. She glanced up and forced a smile.

Dat narrowed his eyes around the room. "You don't fool me. You all have been eavesdropping."

Mum tilted her head up. "Us? We weren't listening. It's hard to hear people who talk in hushed tones."

Dat chuckled and turned to Kathleen. "So you know Dr. Parker is here to see you."

Kathleen set the potato and peeler down. "What does he want?"

Dat shook his head. "I told you. To see you. Now go."

Kathleen resisted the urge to tell her family not to listen, but it would do no *gut*. She walked into the living room.

"Dr. Parker. This is a surprise."

"Doctor? What happened to calling me Ethan?"

Kathleen lowered her voice. "That wouldn't be appropriate."

He matched her lower voice. "Why not?"

"It just wouldn't. You're an *Englisher.*"

"A what?"

"You're not Amish, and you're not a member of my family."

"Ah. You've picked up an accent."

"What? I have?"

"On some of your *Englisher* words."

She cocked her head, not finding his joke funny.

"Your dad invited me to dinner."

Her first impulse was to correct him and say *supper*, but she stopped. It didn't matter what he called the meal. She knew what he was talking about. But why would *Dat* invite him to stay? "What brings you all the way out here?"

"You."

She waited, but when he didn't elaborate, she asked. "Me? Why?"

"I've come to take you back to the city."

"Back to the city? I'm not going back. This is my home."

"I think you'll reconsider when you hear my offer."

"I won't change my mind."

"Can we go outside?" He moved to the door and held it open. "I feel as though we're being listened to. I'm sure we're not, but it would make me feel better anyway."

That was because they were. But no matter what he said to her or what he offered, her family wouldn't judge and would allow her to make her own decision. She went outside anyway. "Nothing you say will change my mind."

He arced one hand through the air and spoke as though he were reading something. "The Dr. Kathleen Yoder Clinic For Underprivileged Children."

Her clinic idea she'd come up with for an assignment? "I don't understand."

"I got Howard to agree to the funding. It'll start out in the hospital. But as it grows, we can move into our own facility."

"We? Our?"

"Yes. You and I. We'll run it together. It's what you always wanted."

It had been an assignment project. But she had believed in it wholeheartedly. Though not for herself. "You misunderstood. What I always wanted was to return home and care for the people in my Amish community."

He shook his head. "How's that working out? Do you have patients crowding your waiting room? Do you even *have* a waiting room?"

"*Ja.* I have a waiting room. And a clinic."

"What about patients? You yourself said it would be hard to get the Amish to trust you as a doctor."

She had patients. Ten of them. So far. Just because most of them were her family members who lived under *Dat* and *Mum*'s roof didn't matter.

"Do your church leaders respect you as a doctor? Do any of your people respect you as a doctor."

Her family did and Noah did. "It's going to take time. Amish are slow to embrace new ideas. But they will come around."

"Until then, what will you do? Take temperatures and bandage scraped knees? You worked really hard to become a doctor. You didn't go through all that work to diagnose colds and dispense ibuprofen. I know you want to be respected as a doctor. This clinic can give you that."

She did want respect as a doctor. She wanted it very much. And the children's clinic could do so much *gut*.

"How long will it take you here to earn even a little bit of respect from a few of these people?"

Longer than she wanted to wait. Her nephew had almost died due to that lack of respect and trust. And come this fall, the leaders would decide if she could even keep her clinic and practice medicine. How could she prove herself if she wasn't truly given the chance? If they turned her down, what then? Never be a doctor? "I don't know. The clinic sounds wonderful, but what about my community here? They still need me."

"You can't help people who don't want to be helped. Help those who want and need your help."

"Why would you take my clinic idea and make it happen? You were one of my strongest opposition."

He gave a wry laugh. "This is a great opportunity. And we could work side by side."

Ethan was offering her the respect she desired. After her brother-in-law had refused her help and Preacher Hochstetler spoke out against her, no one had come to her clinic. Everyone was afraid. Was her little practice ever going to truly be allowed to help anyone? "I don't know."

He smiled. "But you're at least tempted."

She nodded. Maybe *Gott* hadn't wanted her to be a doctor for her community but for underprivileged children. Shouldn't she help where she was both needed and wanted? Maybe that's what *Gott* had called her to do. She wanted to stay in her community. But maybe *Gott* wanted to send her out into the world.

Then she remembered that Noah was coming to supper tonight. She didn't want Ethan and Noah at the same table. She walked toward his car. "I promise to think about it."

He chuckled. "Are you trying to get rid of me?"

She turned back to him. *Ja*, she was. "I need to help my *mum* and sisters with supper preparations."

"Your dad invited me to stay for dinner, remember?"

Of course he did.

Now what was she going to do? Nothing she could do but help with supper and hope Noah forgot.

Noah had hitched up the trap and was now headed to the Yoders. He hoped to entice Kathleen for a buggy ride to try to convince her once again to allow him to court her. As he turned into the Yoders' yard, he automatically pulled back on the reins.

A little red sports car sat parked in front of the house.

Whose car could that be? Obviously an *Englisher*'s. But who? The feeling of a hot coal in the pit of his stomach burned. Someone Kathleen knew. Someone from the outside world. Someone enticing her to leave.

He stared for a long moment, wanting to turn around and leave, then finally put the horse back into motion. After parking by the barn, he meticulously unhitched Fred and turned him out into the corral with David Yoder's three horses.

Time to go inside. It would be rude to keep everyone waiting.

As he climbed the steps, the door opened, and Jessica came out with a worried expression. "You have to do something. An *Englisher* doctor showed up and asked Kathleen to go back with him."

Noah's gut wrenched.

Kathleen wouldn't leave, would she? She'd worked so hard to become a doctor for their people. The community needed her, even if they wouldn't admit it yet. He needed her here. The community needed her. Would there be anything he could say to make her stay? "What did Kathleen say? Did she agree to go with him?"

"She promised to think about it. I don't want her to go away again. Because…this time it would be for *gut*."

He didn't want Kathleen to go away either. "I don't know what I could say to make her stay."

"Ask to court her. I'm sure she'd stay then."

He couldn't tell Jessica he'd already done that and Kathleen had refused him. "That wouldn't make her stay if she doesn't want to."

"*Ja*, it would. She likes you. I can tell."

Could have fooled him. He'd asked, and she'd turned him down faster than his racing heart. Maybe if he told her *vater* that he'd kissed Kathleen, her *vater* would pressure her into courting. Could he do that to her? Would he want her if she'd been forced?

But if she left, that would solve the issue of the kiss. Wouldn't it? He didn't like that solution one bit. She needed to stay, for the community. The community needed her and was long overdue for a doctor. She had to stay. Though she'd only been back for two months, he couldn't imagine life without her here. He'd felt a sense of security knowing she—a doctor—was so close at hand. She couldn't go. There was no way around that. There was no other option. He had to think of a way to make her stay.

He focused his attention back on Jessica's worried face. "The decision is hers. She has been through a lot and done a lot of hard work to become a doctor and return to be a doctor here. She wouldn't give all that up." He hoped his argument soothed her, though it did nothing to assuage his own trepidation.

"She was gone a long time and is as much

English as she is Amish. What if she realizes she likes their way of life better than ours?"

"She's taking the classes and will join church in another month."

"She could easily quit those or even leave after she joins. Joining church is no guarantee she'll stay."

Jessica was right. But he didn't know what else to do. "Let's just see what happens." He opened the screen door for her.

Jessica huffed. "If she leaves, I'm blaming you." Then she entered.

Noah followed. He stared at the man standing with David in the living room. This was worse than he thought. This wasn't some old, crotchety doctor. He was young. Not much older than Kathleen. And if he had to guess, he'd say he might be handsome. Someone a young woman would find handsome and be attracted to. He knew that most Amish tried to seek a spouse who had a *gut* heart and didn't much consider looks. But the English were different. Was Kathleen too English, as Jessica had said? Would she consider this doctor because he was attractive to her?

David turned in Noah's direction and spoke in English. "Ah, Noah. I'm glad you're here. This is Kathleen's friend, Dr. Ethan Parker."

Dr. Parker held out his hand. "Glad to meet you. Call me Ethan."

Noah did not want to shake this man's hand, the man who wanted to take Kathleen away from him, but he did anyway. "Nice to meet you." This would be strange, having a meal with the Yoders and everyone speaking in English.

Kathleen came in from the kitchen. When her gaze met Noah's, a broad smile broke on her face. Her gaze flickered to Dr. Parker, her smile fell and she looked from one to the other.

She'd seemed happy to see Noah. Now she seemed uncomfortable with him here while Dr. Parker was as well. If there was any way for Noah to get out of this meal, he would. Especially for her sake. He didn't want to make her uncomfortable.

Kathleen stumbled over awkward introductions of Noah and Dr. Parker.

Dr. Parker chuckled. "Your father already introduced us."

Noah nodded. "Not to worry." He hoped she understood his message was for her not to worry about him being here while Dr. Parker was.

Everyone sat at the table. David blessed the food—in English—and everyone dished up.

Jessica spoke in *Deutsch*. "We found a family of squirrels in our walnut tree."

David pinned her with a glare and spoke in

Deutsch as well. "You know better than that. We have company. Speak in English. And apologize."

Jessica turned to Dr. Parker and spoke in English. "I'm so sorry. That was rude of me. I forgot to speak in English. Please forgive me." She flashed a smile at Dr. Parker, but Noah could tell it wasn't genuine. She'd spoken in *Deutsch* on purpose. Little imp. It was nice to know she was on his side.

Dr. Parker smiled in return. "No problem."

"All I said was that we found a family of squirrels in our walnut tree."

Dr. Parker glanced around the table. "Do you all usually speak German at your table?"

Kathleen spoke up. "*Ja*, but we all know English very well."

"I took a little German in high school," Dr. Parker said. "Let me see if I can remember any of it."

Of course he did. Dr. Parker was perfect. Dr. Parker could do anything. Dr. Parker could do *everything.*

Dr. Parker switched to German. *"Das...sch... eune schmeckt wunderbar."*

Jessica and Samuel snickered.

Maybe not so perfect after all.

Dr. Parker switched back to English. "Did I muck that all up? What did I say?"

Noah had to admit that Dr. Parker was a likable fellow. Hard to dislike.

When no one translated what the man had said, Samuel jumped in with the translation. "This barn tastes wonderful."

Dr. Parker laughed at his own ineptitude. "I barely passed the class."

Very difficult to dislike.

After dessert, Dr. Parker stood. "I hate to eat and run, but I should go. *Danki*." He turned to Kathleen. "See me out?"

Kathleen glanced at Noah before she faced her *vater*.

Noah willed him to say *ne*.

But he nodded.

Kathleen glanced at Noah again before she left with Dr. Parker.

Noah's gut wrenched this way and that. He assumed supper had tasted *wunderbar* as Dr. Parker had said. All of Pamela's meals were, but tonight's had tasted like chalk and roiled in his stomach. He shouldn't have eaten so much. Shouldn't have eaten at all. Shouldn't have come.

He wanted to leave quickly before Kathleen came back, but that would mean seeing Kathleen and Dr. Parker together outside. There would be no way to get past them without being seen. He was stuck.

But in only a couple of minutes, he heard the sound of an engine starting and tires crunching in the dirt driveway, and then Kathleen returned inside. She gave him a shy smile.

Noah stood. "I need to go as well."

Kathleen almost appeared disappointed. "I'll walk you out." She didn't even bother to gain permission from her *vater* like she had with Dr. Parker. What did that mean? Did she want to tell him she'd accepted Dr. Parker's offer? He didn't want to hear that.

"You don't have to."

"I want to." She hurried to the door.

He held the door and walked with her in silence out to the corral.

"I'm sorry about Dr. Parker being here. I had no idea he would show up."

"You can't control what others do." He understood that better than most he supposed, considering the present situation.

She glanced at the trap. "You drove here?"

He nodded. He understood her confusion. He usually walked or rode bareback.

"Why?"

"Why did I drive instead of walking?"

She nodded.

Because I wanted to take you for a buggy ride. "I just felt like driving. The trap was already hitched." Because he'd hitched it to come see her.

"Now I feel even worse."

"Why?"

"I suspect you planned to ask me for a buggy ride. Have you changed your mind?"

He walked Fred from the corral and hitched him to the trap. "I didn't figure you'd want to, with the doctor having been here. I know he asked you to go back with him."

She jerked around to him. "You do? How?"

"Jessica overheard."

"You aren't going to tell my *dat*, are you?"

"It's not my place. But I can't vouch for your sister."

"I'll talk to her."

"Are you going to go?"

"I told him I'd think about it."

That wrenched his insides. She was actually considering his offer.

She put one hand on the trap. "I know why you wanted to take me on a buggy ride."

"You do?" He wasn't quite sure himself.

"You wanted to talk me into courting. I don't want to hurt you, but as I said before, I don't ever plan to marry. I can't."

It would be difficult to be a wife, *mutter and* doctor. At least in an Amish community. English women did it all the time. Did Kathleen long to be English so she could be all three?

"If I asked you to still go on a buggy ride with me, would you?"

Her sweet smile tugged at her mouth. "Why are you asking me? It's my *dat* you need to get permission from."

That was a *ja*. "I'll be right back." He jogged off toward the house.

Her *vater* readily gave his permission, as Noah knew he would. Kathleen's *vater* would rather have Kathleen courted by an Amish man than risk her leaving home again. For *gut*.

When he came back out, Kathleen sat on the trap seat with the reins in her hands.

"You were that sure he'd say *ja*?"

She answered with a smile. "Are you coming?" She held the reins aloft as though she was about to put the buggy in motion.

He jumped in and sat next to her.

She offered him the reins.

He waved them away. "You drive."

"Me? I haven't driven much in years."

"Then this will be *gut* practice." He leaned back in the seat.

She flicked the reins and giggled as the horse pulled the trap into motion.

"It'll come back to you." It wasn't like driving a car. And if she ran into any difficulty, he could give her gentle instructions. But he didn't foresee her having any trouble.

His mind circled around to driving a car. Had Dr. Parker ever let her drive his fancy red car? Had he given her lessons? Noah didn't want to think about the man being that close to Kathleen.

"So if you never plan to marry, why are you considering Dr. Parker's proposal? Isn't that kind of giving him false hope?"

She guided Fred onto the country road. "What does marriage have to do with it?"

Now he was confused. "Isn't that what his offer is? A proposal of marriage?"

Kathleen jerked her gaze to his. "Certainly not. Is that what Jessica told you?"

He thought back to his conversation with her sister. *Ne*, she hadn't said anything about marriage. "She said he asked you to come back with him, and you agreed to think about it."

Kathleen shook her head. "I'll have to remember to move farther away from the house when I have private conversations."

There weren't many secrets in an Amish community.

"The reason he wants me to return is to open a clinic for disadvantaged children. It was a project assignment we worked on as residents."

"But I thought you wanted to be a doctor here?"

"*I* do, but that doesn't mean the community will allow me to. What if *Gott* wanted me to become a doctor to help these children and that's why it's so difficult to be accepted here? What if it was just me wanting to come back and not *Gott*'s will at all? Out there, I could be respected as a doctor. If I'm not allowed to use my hard-earned skills, why did I go through all that trouble? I don't know what to do anymore."

Stay, he wanted to scream. "A man like Dr. Parker wants you back for more than working at a clinic for children."

She gave a little laugh. "You mean like marriage? *Ne.* He's always very professional."

"*Ja*, I mean marriage. He could open a clinic with any doctors. But he came out all this way to ask you."

"That's because I was in the group with him."

"He could have written. That would have been more businesslike."

She was quiet.

So he went on. "I saw the way he looked at you. Trying to fit in with your family."

"I hardly think he wants to be Amish. And he didn't *look* at me in any special way. It's the way he always looks at all people."

She couldn't see it. She truly couldn't see it.

"I don't mean to be disagreeable, but he didn't

look at anyone else around the table the way he gazed at you."

She pulled the horse over to the side of the road and stopped. She shifted in the seat to face him. "You're serious, aren't you? You think he wants to marry me?"

"Ja."

She turned back forward and stared. "I... I don't know what to say."

Say you won't go.

She faced him again. "You don't think that's why I'm considering his offer, do you? I'm only considering it to be respected as a doctor."

That was *gut* to know. But the marriage aspect might appeal to her and tip her in Dr. Parker's direction. She could have everything with him. He needed to find a way to stop that. "You know how slow to accept change our people are. It will take time, but I believe they'll come to accept you as a doctor. You can pave the way for others who want to do *gut* and help our community in unconventional ways. Don't give up too easily."

After a moment, she nudged the trap back onto the road. "May I change the subject?"

"Sure."

"I don't think you need to feel like we must court because we kissed. No one knows and nothing really happened. I don't see anything wrong in it."

"That's because you lived in the English world so long. They see things differently."

"You really think of this as a big issue?"

"I do. We have *hands-off* courtships here."

"Not everyone chooses that."

He had hoped she wouldn't remember that. "But most do. If anyone found out, we would be frowned upon."

"Well, I'm not going to tell anyone. Are you?"

He might need to. "That wouldn't change what happened."

She pulled into his driveway.

"What are you doing?"

"I'll walk back home."

"*Ne*, you won't." He couldn't allow her to walk home alone at dusk. He held out his hands for the reins. Would she give up the reins? Would she make a fuss about him taking her home?

With a huge sigh, she handed them over.

It was *gut* to know she could be reasonable.

Now, would she be reasonable enough to stay here where she belonged?

Chapter Eleven

The following morning after breakfast, Kathleen followed *Dat* and her brothers out the side kitchen door. "Benjamin?"

The oldest of her brothers stopped and turned. *"Ja."*

Kathleen quickened her steps to meet up with him in the yard. "May I borrow your courting buggy today?"

His courting buggy was the same open-air variety as Noah's two-wheeled trap. "Sure. Are you leaving right away?"

"Soon."

"I'll hitch it up for you before I leave."

"Danki." Kathleen ran back inside.

Jessica stood in her path. "I'm ready to leave whenever you are."

Kathleen hadn't thought about how to keep Jessica from going with her today. She could make the call from her office and leave Jessica at the clinic. "Be ready in five minutes."

"I'm ready now."

Mum laughed. "It looks like Jessica is back to that little girl who couldn't be parted from you."

Kathleen loved her sister and loved that she wanted to be with her, but today, she would have to cope with a few hours of separation. "I love having her with me." She would set Jessica to work at a task in the clinic.

A few minutes later, Benjamin came in. "The buggy is tied out front."

She hadn't wanted anyone to know. Too late. *"Danki."*

"Buggy?" *Mum* said.

"I didn't feel like walking today." Because she was going all the way into town and *that* would be a long walk indeed.

"Didn't you sleep well last night? I thought your sleeping was getting better."

It had been better than when she first arrived. Now she was getting a *gut* six hours in a row. Except last night. What Noah had told her about Ethan had disturbed her, her thoughts galloping through her mind about the disadvantaged children's clinic Ethan had offered her. A chance to be respected as a doctor. "I didn't sleep as well as I have been. I kept waking up. My body is still adjusting to more normal sleep. I will be fine." Once she talked to Ethan and cleared up any misconceptions.

"All right. Have a *gut* day."

Thankful *Mum* had not questioned her further or detained her, she turned to Jessica. "Pack us a lunch and meet me at the buggy."

"All right." Jessica got to work.

Kathleen went to her room and gathered her things, along with Ethan's business card he'd given her last night just before he left. She should get business cards.

A few minutes later, Kathleen and her sister were seated in the buggy and on their way. She pulled into Noah's driveway and up to the clinic. She thrilled at the sight of the sign Noah had made her, as always. She might not have patients yet, but she had a door sign with her name.

Noah. She hoped this was one of the days he was busy elsewhere. She didn't want to face him until after she'd spoken to Ethan. Even then, she might not want to see Noah. It would depend on what happened in town.

She set the brake, wrapped the reins around the handle and climbed out.

Jessica stepped down and grabbed the lunch basket. "Do you want me to unhitch the horse?"

That would be the thing to do if she weren't going into town. "Not just yet."

Kathleen went inside ahead of her baby sister. As she walked through the waiting area toward her office, she said, "Could you give this whole area a thorough cleaning?" Not that she expected any patients. She'd had only one or two patients a week with minor things to treat: sore throat, burn, scrapes and one case taken care of with butterfly adhesive strips. Her most difficult case to date. But she needed to keep her sister busy. She continued on into her office and shut the door. Something she didn't normally do.

She sat behind the desk and stared at the phone. She picked up the handset and stared at the numbers. Then she slipped Ethan's business card out of her side seam dress pocket.

At the soft knock on the door and the turn of the handle, she clumsily and a bit noisily replaced the handset and secreted the business card onto her lap. *"Ja."*

Jessica poked her head around the door. "Do you want me to scrub the kitchen floor or just sweep it?"

Kathleen didn't know and didn't really care. "If it's fine with only a sweeping, then don't bother to mop. But if it looks like it needs it, then please do."

"All right." She disappeared and shut the door without a sound.

If Kathleen wanted to get her call made uninterrupted, she needed to be quick about it. She picked up the handset again and retrieved the card. She flipped it over to where Ethan had written his cell phone number.

She wished she knew where he was staying so she could call and leave a message at the front desk. Taking a deep breath, she punched in the numbers.

Ring number one.

Her stomach tightened.

Number two.

Her chest tightened.

Three.

Her breathing became shallow. She wanted to hang up, but he would just call the number back from the caller ID. And she certainly didn't want Jessica picking up.

Four?

Where was he? If he'd turned his phone off, it would have gone straight to voice mail.

Then the slight click of the phone being answered with a sleepy "Hello—" Then a clunking and clacking that sounded as though the phone might have been dropped.

"Hello?" she ventured.

More clacking and scratching sounds, then Ethan came back on the line with another sleepy "Hello?"

At least she thought it was him. "Ethan? This is Kathleen Yoder."

He cleared his throat, and his voice seemed to wake up. "Kathleen? I wasn't expecting you to call."

Then why had he given her his phone number? "Did I wake you up?"

"No. Of course not. Okay. Yes, you did. You know how it is with irregular sleeping schedules that are always changing. I slept for a couple of hours, then was up for several, and then I dropped off again around six. But you didn't call to hear about that. Have you decided to accept my offer?"

"I would like to talk to you about that."

"Sure. What do you want to know?"

"Not on the phone. There is a coffee shop on the corner of Chicago Avenue and Lincoln Highway. Can you meet me there at ten?"

"Of course. But I can come pick you up. Then we could meet sooner."

That wouldn't do. "No, ten will be fine. I'll meet you then. Goodbye."

"Kathleen?"

"Ja."

His voice took on a wistful quality. "I'm really glad you called."

Her insides flopped. She didn't know how to

respond to that. Fortunately, she didn't have to because he spoke again.

"See you at ten." He hung up, and so did she.

She hoped this was the right course of action. Leaving now would allow her to make the hour and a half drive and arrive before ten. She wanted to be seated and ready. The last one to a meeting was at a disadvantage.

After leaving her office, she found Jessica crouching with the broom in one hand and the dustpan in the other, corralling the dirt from the floor into the dustpan.

Jessica straightened and dumped the dirt into the waste pail. "I don't think the floor needs to be mopped. What do you think?"

Kathleen glanced at the floor. It did look fine. Why shouldn't it? It had been walked on very little since the last time it was mopped. Jessica didn't need to do unnecessary work, but at the same time, she wanted to keep her sister busy. "It looks fine. I'm going into town. I'll be back by lunch."

Jessica quickly tucked the broom back into the utility closet. "Oh *gut*. I'd love to go into town."

Not what Kathleen had planned. "I was going to go alone."

"Oh, please let me go with you. I love going

into town. *Mum* thinks I like too much about town and doesn't like me to go."

Mum was probably right. And if *Mum* didn't want Jessica going all the time, it was best if Kathleen didn't take her. "How do you think *Mum* will react when she learns I took you into town without her permission?"

"I won't tell her." Then her face brightened. "*That's* the reason you drove the buggy."

Her little sister was perceptive. "I don't—"

The front door opened, and Kathleen whirled around.

Noah entered. "Would you like me to unhitch your horse?"

"*Ne. Danki.* I'm heading into town."

"I can go with you."

Not Noah too. Was that hope she heard in his voice?

Jessica latched onto Kathleen's arm. "Sorry. I'm going with her. Benjamin's buggy doesn't seat more than two."

Given the choice between the two, Jessica would be the better one for the errand Kathleen needed to make.

Noah nodded. "Then I'll see you later." The hope gone from his voice.

Kathleen wanted it back. "We should be back for lunch. If you're around, you can join us. We have plenty of food."

His face brightened. "I'll see you then."

All three walked out, and Noah held on to the harness while Kathleen and Jessica climbed aboard.

"Can I drive?" Jessica reached for the reins.

Kathleen laughed. "I'll drive. I need the practice."

Noah waved as Kathleen drove off. She nodded in reply.

Jessica waved to Noah, then situated herself forward. "He likes you, you know?"

"Who?" Her sister couldn't mean Ethan. How would she know? Did she suspect Kathleen was going to meet him? How would she excuse herself from Jessica?

Jessica guffawed. "Noah, silly."

"Noah?"

How could Jessica know that? Had she seen Noah kiss her? This could not be *gut*.

"He hangs around the clinic. He looks at you a lot. And he acts happier now that you're home."

Noah certainly didn't care for her in that way. But the thought made her giddy inside anyway. *Ne.* She needed to stop that. She could never marry, and that was that. She would have to put Noah Lambright right out of her mind.

She had assumed that Noah had asked to court her only because he'd kissed her as he said. And he'd only kissed her because she'd been so upset. But had that all been an excuse? Hadn't he said that he never planned to marry?

At the edge of town, Kathleen knew she needed to part from her sister. "Can I drop you at the library?"

"So you can meet Dr. Parker?"

"What? How did you know about that?"

"I heard you on the phone."

"It's nothing. I'm just meeting him for coffee. I'll let you off at the library."

"*Gut.* I want to check out some books on business."

When Kathleen pulled to a stop in front of the library, she put her hand on her baby sister's arm. "Please reconsider going to college. What do you want to study business for?"

"So I can learn to run a successful business."

But would the lure of the outside world be too much for Jessica to resist? Would Kathleen's disobedience cause her sister to stumble and leave their community? She wouldn't be able to forgive herself for that.

Jessica flashed a smile, like she did when she was a baby. "Don't worry about me." She climbed down.

"I'll be back by ten thirty." Her conversation with Ethan shouldn't take long.

Jessica nodded and waved, then disappeared through the library doors.

Kathleen clucked the horse into motion. She would need to hurry if she was going to arrive before Ethan.

She pulled up to the coffee shop ten minutes early. She went inside to find Ethan already seated at a table in the far corner.

He waved her over.

He was early?

She hadn't anticipated that. So much for getting herself a cup of coffee.

With his charming smile, he stood as she approached the table and held a chair out for her.

She sat across from him.

He waved to the barista before seating himself again. "Your coffee will be here in a minute."

"My coffee? But I haven't ordered anything."

"I ordered it ahead of time."

"*Danki*—I mean thank you. You didn't have to do that."

"I know how much we doctors live on coffee. Some days I wish I could have a caffeine IV drip. Say fifty milligrams an hour."

Kathleen didn't have the heart to tell him that she'd cut way back on her consumption. But with her lack of sleep last night, she could use it.

The coffees arrived. Two extra larges.

She inhaled the aroma. Strong, dark and loaded with sugar. "You had them add sugar."

"Three heaping teaspoons. I know you like yours sweet."

He remembered? This wasn't *gut*. He was too cheerful and happy to see her. Trying too hard. "You didn't have to wait for me to get your coffee."

He dipped his head, then looked up sideways, sheepishly. "This is my third."

"How long have you been here?"

"Since five after nine. I wanted to make sure I didn't miss you."

Well, he'd made sure of that. So, no matter how early she'd intended to arrive, he still would have been here before her. She sat awkwardly for a minute.

He cleared his throat. "Please tell me you're going to accept my offer and work with me at the clinic."

"I haven't decided." The idea appealed to her. A lot. She would have no trouble getting patients or being respected. But she would have to leave her people for *gut*. And leave Noah. Her breath caught.

"Then why did you want to talk to me?"

She might as well dive right in. "Someone said that your offer was for more than just working at the clinic."

He shifted in his chair and studied his coffee. "Like what?"

She felt foolish saying it but couldn't back out now. "Like your offer might include more than working at the clinic."

"More?" He took a long sip of his coffee as though he were hiding behind it.

If she decided to accept his offer, she needed to know exactly where she stood. "Me."

He set his cup down and took several deep breaths, gazing at her.

Ne. Noah had been right.

Ethan stretched out his hand and rested it on hers. "You had to know I care about you. I pushed for the clinic for you."

This was what she'd been afraid of. She slipped her hand from his. "You know I'm never going to get married. I can't be a doctor and a wife. It can't be done."

"Not with the Amish. But out here—" he spread his hands wide "—it's done all the time."

That was true. Could she actually have a career as a doctor as well as being a wife and *mutter*?

He reached across the table and recaptured her hand in both of his. "I care a lot for you. I might even go so far as to say that I love you."

"Don't say that." She knew she didn't love him. But she loved what he was offering her. Something no Amish man could. Or would. Besides, *Englishers* threw around the word *love* like it was nothing more than a chocolate candy to be savored for the moment then on to the next thing they loved. It wasn't something lasting.

"If you accept the position at the clinic, I won't pressure you. We can date like everyone else, and you can let your feelings for me grow."

He assumed they would. Would they? In Amish marriages, there wasn't always love when a couple married. But it always grew after marriage. Didn't it?

"I don't know. I'll think about it. About all of it." She stood, pulling her hand free again.

He stood as well. "Don't go. I feel as though I just messed everything up between us."

"You have given me a lot to consider. I need time."

"How much time? I just want to know when I should stop hoping."

"Next month I must make the decision to join church or not. I'll let you know by then."

"Just so you know, if you accept the clinic position, I won't assume I'm part of that. I'll give you all the time you need."

She appreciated that, nodded and left without so much as one sip of her coffee.

It was only ten o'clock. Too early to pick up Jessica.

So she stopped by a big box store to pick up

supplies for her clinic. She had to have something to prove she went into town with a purpose other than to see Ethan.

After that, she headed to the library, parked and went inside. Heddy wasn't sitting behind the desk. Nor did she see the woman as Kathleen searched for her sister.

Jessica checked out an armload of books, several on business and two on getting a GED. Should Kathleen tell her parents? Or let this play out and see where it led? Maybe her sister would grow tired of the idea. After helping with the plethora, Kathleen drove back to her clinic.

"How did your meeting go with Dr. Parker?" Jessica asked.

How did it go? "All right, I guess."

"What did he want?"

What should she tell her sister? Until she made a decision, it was best not to tell her anything. "Nothing really."

Jessica's voice took on a concerned quality. "Are you going leave again? For *gut*?"

"Ne." The word shot out of Kathleen's mouth before she knew it. Was that how she truly felt? Or just a practiced response due to years of conditioning? "I don't know. I always dreamed of coming back and helping our community."

"But no one is making that easy for you."

"*Ne*, they're not." Except Noah. "Don't say anything to anyone. All right?" Especially Noah.

"All right. But I'm going to be praying for you to stay. Forever."

Chapter Twelve

Noah sat at his *vater*'s kitchen table, cradling a cup of coffee in his hands. He couldn't shake the feeling of needing to talk to his *mutter*. The only person who really knew about her was his *vater*. Which had propelled him here. But he didn't know how to bring up the subject. His *vater* only ever talked about Noah's *mutter* in general terms, but mostly avoided the subject.

His *vater* cradled his own cup. "I can't remember the last time you sat at my table."

"It's been a while." Though they saw each other every other week at church service and sometimes in between, they didn't see each other on a regular basis.

Staring into his coffee, his *vater* spoke. "When a man gets on in years, he thinks back over his life and can see his mistakes clearly. One of my biggest regrets is pushing you away."

"You never pushed me away."

"I did by being harsh with you. I promised myself that if I ever had the blessing of having you at my table again, I'd let you know I was sorry. Sorry for a lot of things."

His *vater* had always seemed strong and self-assured. But the man before Noah looked humbled. Maybe his *vater* was ready to talk about Noah's *mutter*. "Why did *Mutter* leave?"

He stared into his coffee. "Another regret. I did and said things when I was younger that were unkind and unfair. I couldn't see what I had. Only what I *didn't* have."

"I remember you and *Mutter* fighting, but I never saw you hit her or anything. Nothing that would give her reason to leave."

His *vater* took a deep breath before speaking again. "The wounds I inflicted and the scars I created were on the inside. On her heart."

Noah waited for his *vater* to go on.

"I know you want me to tell you the rest, but it's your *mutter*'s story to tell, not mine. If she's in town, you should go talk to her."

"I don't know what to say to her after all these years."

"Ask her to explain, and then just listen."

"So you're not going to tell me anything."

"After you speak to her, if you still have questions, I'll see what I can answer. But you need to talk with her first."

This had not been very helpful. Noah stood, went out to the corral and retrieved his horse.

As he swung up onto his horse, his *vater* came to his side. "Two things, Noah. No matter what your *mutter* tells you, I do love you, son."

"I've never doubted your love." But his *vater* feared he might. "And the second thing?"

"I've never stopped loving her either."

He still loved *Mutter*?

"Would you welcome her back after all these years?"

"I might."

That was unexpected. But it shouldn't be. The Amish forgave no matter the transgression if the guilty party confessed and asked for forgiveness. Would his *mutter* be willing?

Noah worked in his barn on a filing cabinet for Kathleen. He had sanded the wood smooth. When she had more patient records, she would need a place to store them. He had to believe she would have more patients. She had to. If not, she might be tempted by Dr. Parker's offer to leave.

When he heard barking, Noah peeked out of the barn.

All three dogs ran out to greet the incoming buggy.

His heart relaxed at the sight of Kathleen.

He went back inside and threw a canvas tarp over the filing cabinet. He wanted it to be a surprise.

Then he strolled over to the *dawdy haus* to unhitch her horse. He took hold of the harness. "I'll take care of her and then be in for lunch. If the offer still stands."

Kathleen gifted him with a genuine smile. Not the forced one she'd had before she left. "Of course. We'll get everything set out." She grabbed several plastic bags by the handles.

Jessica hoisted a tall stack of what appeared to be library books. "Don't be long."

He didn't intend to. "Can I get those for you? Either of you?"

"We have them," Jessica said. *"Danki."*

She seemed eager.

He wondered why, though it really didn't matter. Jessica wasn't the only one who wanted him to hurry. He longed to sit in Kathleen's company.

Once the horse was settled in the corral, he went inside. The table had been set with a white tablecloth, plates and flatware. A little fancy for a picnic-style lunch.

Jessica grinned. "Have a seat. I'll tell Kathleen everything is ready." She sauntered to her sister's office, looking back over her shoulder. She motioned for him to sit.

He did and stared at the table.

Jessica had made a mistake. There were only two plates set out.

Maybe he wasn't welcome at lunch after all. He would just get another plate. But he was too late.

Jessica returned with Kathleen.

He stood anyway.

Pulling out a chair, Jessica spoke to her sister. "Have a seat."

Kathleen sat. "Certainly we don't need plates. And there's one short."

"I'll get it," Noah said.

Jessica waved him away. "Don't bother. I have to go back home. I remembered something *Mum* needed help with this afternoon. Bye." She scooped up her books and darted out the door.

Kathleen jerked her head back. "What was that all about?" Though her expression told him she knew.

Noah chuckled and sat back down. "Not very subtle."

"*Ne*, she's not. I'm sorry about her."

"Don't be."

"We can pretend this is just an ordinary lunch like we've shared many times, can't we?"

Ordinary? There was nothing ordinary about

Kathleen. "Sure." He said a blessing over the meal, and they ate in companionable silence.

When Kathleen served him a piece of peach cobbler, he said, "Can I ask you a question?"

She smiled. "Of course."

He wanted to get lost in her smile but turned his thoughts back to his question. "Earlier, when you left for town, you seemed uneasy around me. Did I do something? Or was it because of last night?"

"Ne—ja—ne—"

What had made her so flustered? "I don't mean to upset you."

"You haven't. You haven't done anything. And *ja*, it does have to do with last night." She was silent for a few moments.

"You don't have to tell me if you don't want to."

"Ne. You deserve to know. I didn't sleep well thinking about what you said."

He wanted to ask which thing that he said had disturbed her so much but decided to wait for her to tell him on her own.

"I just couldn't see what you saw where Eth— Dr. Parker was concerned."

He didn't want to think or talk about Dr. Parker.

"It made no sense that he had anything more in mind than a position at the new clinic."

But he had.

"I went into town to talk to him. He admitted he…has feelings for me."

She seemed sort of upset, but not fully. Did this revelation change her mind? "So have you reconsidered thinking over his offer?"

"I'm still considering it."

Ne!

"I would have real patients that would *want* me to treat them. I'd be respected as a doctor."

And she would have Dr. Parker. Noah wished he'd never told her that the *Englisher* doctor had more in mind than just a clinic. He'd thought it would turn her off the idea. But it hadn't. He pushed back from the table and to his feet. "I have work to do."

Kathleen stood as well. "What about your cobbler?"

"I'm full. *Danki* for the food." He strode out, off the porch and into the barn.

He'd been a fool to think the Amish way of life could compete with everything Dr. Parker could offer Kathleen. She'd been young when she left and had been gone so long that it was natural for her to think more like an *Englisher* than an Amish. *Ja*, after all that time, she could never truly think like an Amish again.

He pulled the tarp back from the file cabinet. Should he bother to even finish it? She wasn't likely to stay. He kicked it with his boot and dented the wood on the bottom.

"Noah?"

At the sound of Kathleen's voice, he jerked the tarp back into place and spun around. *"Ja."* He walked toward the entrance where she stood.

"I feel as though I should apologize for upsetting you."

"You have nothing to apologize for."

"But you seem upset that I went to see Ethan."

Why did she have to use his first name? It was too familiar. Dr. Parker was an outsider. "You are free to see whomever you like. I'm upset that you're considering his offer. What happened to helping our community? What about everything you went through? What about your sister Nancy? Was all that just an excuse? Was I wrong to stand up for you to the other church leaders?" Had he been wrong to allow his feelings to grow for her?

"They don't want me as a doctor here."

"So you are just going to give up after three months? You knew it was going to be hard. You knew it would take time and convincing. You said you would have to convince our community. Where did all your aspirations go? This community needs you, whether they want to admit it or not. What about your nephew? Without you, he would have suffered the same fate as your sister."

Her eyes filled with tears.

He hadn't meant to hurt her. He'd just wanted her to come to her senses. "I'm sorry. I shouldn't have said all those things."

She shook her head. "Don't be sorry. Everything you said is true. I'll hitch up my horse and leave."

He stepped toward her. "Don't go, Kathleen. Please."

"I have a lot to think about."

"You can't do that at home with your *mutter* and sisters around. You know Jessica will pester you as to why you are home already. Stay at the *dawdy haus* for the afternoon. I promise not to bother you."

After a moment, she nodded and walked away.

A part of him went with her. And he realized, a part of him would always go with her.

Kathleen went back to the *dawdy haus*. She had much to consider and think over. Everything Noah had said was true.

Where had all of her hopes and dreams gone? Where *had* her aspirations gone? Where had her convictions gone?

Lord, what should I do?

She spent the afternoon flip-flopping between trying to figure out what to do and worrying that Noah would come and try to sway her to stay. Then there was always the disappointment when he hadn't come. He'd been true to his word. And the solitude of the house did offer her a quiet place and the time to think.

But now that it was time to go home, she hoped Noah didn't try to talk her into anything or ask her if she'd made a decision. Because she hadn't. She was no closer to knowing what she was going to do than four hours ago.

Maybe she could slip out and walk home without him noticing. But what about the horse and Benjamin's buggy? *Ne*, she couldn't leave them here. That would be irresponsible. If Noah was anywhere around when she hitched up the horse and buggy, she prayed he wouldn't pressure her.

She collected her backpack of traveling medical supplies and the picnic basket. Lunch had been a disaster. She opened the door, stepped out onto the porch and stopped.

Tied to the porch railing stood her horse hitched to her brother's buggy.

She looked around.

Noah was nowhere to be seen.

He'd been true to his word and thoughtful to boot.

She locked the clinic and stowed her things in the buggy before climbing aboard. As she drove out of his driveway and turned onto the road, she glanced back but still didn't see Noah.

She arrived home way too quickly for her liking. When had buggy travel seemed so fast? She could use more time to herself.

Neither *Dat* nor her brothers were in the barn, so she unhitched the horse and turned him out into the corral, then she wheeled the buggy into its place in the barn.

When Kathleen entered the house through the kitchen door, *Mum* glanced up from cutting biscuit dough and did a double take. "Gracious, Kathleen. You look peaked. Are you feeling all right?"

"*Ja.* I'm fine." Though she did feel absolutely drained, between little sleep and the upheaval of her emotions. "I'll put my things away and come back down to help."

"You lay down and rest. We have supper well in hand."

Kathleen climbed the stairs.

In her wake came Jessica. "Did you have a fight with Noah?"

Kathleen wouldn't call it a fight, exactly. She shook her head. "Don't think we both don't know what you were up to by setting the table like that and leaving so conspicuously."

Her baby sister grinned. "Did it work?"

Kathleen offered a withering look. "What do you think?" She didn't need her sister playing matchmaker.

Jessica straightened. "I think I need to try harder."

"Don't bother. I don't plan to ever marry. I gave up that option when I decided to become a doctor."

Jessica's expression changed to concern. "Why?"

"No Amish man is going to want their wife busy being a doctor."

"No *Amish* man? Is that why you met with Dr. Parker? Are you going to marry him?"

"I haven't made any decisions yet."

"So you're considering marrying him?"

"Ne." At least Kathleen didn't think so.

"Noah would let you be a doctor. I know he would."

Would he? Even if he would, he deserved better than a wife who would be busy with patients all day and might be gone at all hours. "He doesn't wish to marry again. So your little matchmaking schemes won't work."

"But—"

"Please let me rest."

Jessica huffed as she left the room.

Kathleen flopped back onto her bed. Life had

been so much easier as an Amish before she left. Now it seemed as though every time she turned around, her life was getting more and more complicated.

Noah had kissed her and wanted to court because of it. If she said *ja*, he would eventually offer her marriage. If she married him, what would become of all her medical training?

And Ethan wanted her to go back to the English world with him. And marry him? Out there she could be a doctor *and* a wife. But did she want that? Did she want to marry Ethan?

But what about Noah? He'd stood up for her and helped her get her clinic going. If she left, she would disappoint him.

She had a lot to think about.

Chapter Thirteen

Two days later, Noah jumped down from his covered buggy in the Yoders' yard. He had made a decision. He was going to see his *mutter*. And he wanted Kathleen to come along. Not because he needed her there when he spoke to his *mutter* for the first time in over a decade and a half. Not because she'd talked to his *mutter* already. And not because he need a mediator.

He wanted her along simply because he enjoyed her company. But if he was being honest with himself, her support would encourage him. And with her beside him, he wouldn't be able to change his mind.

As he climbed the porch steps, Jessica came out the door. "Noah. We weren't expecting you. Kathleen and I were just about to head over to the clinic."

"I have a favor to ask you. Don't head over until the afternoon. I'm taking Kathleen into town."

Jessica wiggled her eyebrows, leaned close and lowered her voice. "Does she know that?"

He chuckled. "Not yet."

She put one hand on her hip. "How do you feel about Ada Mae Hershberger being a *mutter* of five and running her Plain & Simple shop of Amish novelties?" Her voice took on a wistful quality, and she no longer looked at him. "And Sarah Kuhns runs a fruit stand with her children. And Hannah Lapp does custom quilting, and she has children. You don't have anything against a wife and *mutter* helping contribute to the family, do you?"

"Ne." He wasn't sure what Jessica was going on about, but felt as though he was answering more than her straightforward question. "Is Kathleen here?"

"I'll go get her."

"Danki."

Jessica dashed inside and spoke in a singsong voice. "Kathleen, there's a dashing man waiting for you on the porch."

That girl needed to learn to be a little more subtle.

When Kathleen came out, she wore a concerned expression that quickly brightened. "Oh. It's you."

"Who were you expecting?"

"No one. I mean I wasn't expecting anyone first thing in the morning. Jessica and I are just on our way to the clinic."

From inside the house, Jessica called, "I'm going to head over after lunch. So you two go on without me."

Kathleen opened her mouth to reply, but Noah spoke first. "I asked her to come over later."

"Oh. I can come over later as well if there's a problem."

"No problem. I just wanted you to go into town with me."

She narrowed her eyes and stepped back. "Why?"

He had two reasons and neither were the one he would give her. "I'm going to visit my *mutter*. I'd like to have you along."

She straightened. "Oh. I'd be happy to. But you don't need me to go with you. She was very nice."

Noah thought back and remembered his *mutter* being a kind and caring woman. "I'd like you there."

"Then I'd be happy to go. Let me get my things."

He'd had the dream again, but when he rounded the corner, his *mutter was* there… With Kathleen at her side.

In no time, Kathleen sat at *his* side as he drove into town. So the first reason for inviting her was accomplished. Now for the second. "Have you made a decision about Dr. Parker's offer?"

Kathleen remained silent for a minute. "I don't want to talk about his offer or him. But *ne*, I haven't decided."

Well, at least she hadn't chosen to leave. "All right, but I'd like to say one thing, then I'll drop it."

"What's that?"

"You left and went to college with a clear purpose, to return and help our people. I don't believe that has changed. If our people didn't need a doctor so badly, you never would have left. But they did then and still do now."

"They need a doctor who can help them. I'm not so sure I'm that doctor. If no one will come to me, then I'm useless here, and it would be better that there were no doctor than an ineffective one. It would be better for an *Englisher* doctor to be brought in than to have me standing in the way of help for this community."

He noticed she didn't say *my* or *our* community. Was she detaching herself? "I believe you are meant to be *our* doctor."

"But how many people have to die before the leaders come around? I don't want to be responsible for people dying because I'm an impediment for another doctor coming in to practice. Can we please drop this now?"

He didn't want to because he hadn't convinced her to stay yet, but he would, because she asked. If he pushed any further, she might jump out and walk back.

The silence that hung in the air became strained. He wanted to ease the unspoken tension. "You asked me if I was angry with you for talking to my *mutter* without asking me."

"I should have asked you first."

"*Ne.* It's not mine to say who you can speak to." He'd taken his *mutter* not being home last time as a sign from *Gott* that he didn't need to reconcile with her. She'd made her choice and it was up to her to take the first step. But after Kathleen had visited her, he'd had this odd feeling. It took him a few days to figure out what it was. *She'd* talked his *mutter*, and now he wanted to. "I'm a bit envious that you have gotten to speak to her and I haven't."

"And you're changing that today."

He still didn't know what to say to her. Should he just blurt out, *Why did you leave us? Why did you leave me?* That was the crux of it. He'd felt abandoned. And why the thought of Kathleen considering leaving felt like she was abandoning him too, even though he knew he had no history or real connection with her.

When they pulled into town, Noah's insides felt all twisted up. "You said she works at the library?"

"It won't be open yet. You'll have better luck if you go to her house."

He pulled up in front of the little cottage about the size of the *dawdy haus*. He didn't get out.

But Kathleen did. "Are you coming?"

"I don't know." He wanted to say just the right thing to his *mutter*.

"No hurry." She leaned against the side of the buggy and waited.

After a few minutes, the front door opened, and an Amish woman stepped out onto the small porch but no farther. His *mutter*.

Pushing away from the rig, Kathleen glanced between *mutter* and son. "She'll speak to you. I know she will."

"But will I be able to speak to her?"

"She's your *mutter*. The words will come."

Would they? "You go. I'll be along in a minute."

She nodded and headed up the walk to the porch. They spoke, but he couldn't tell what they said.

His *mutter* gave him a nod and disappeared inside with Kathleen.

He wanted to say mean things to her. Accuse her of her misdeeds. Hurl pent-up questions and frustrations at her. Make her feel the pain he felt the first time she left. And the second. And the third and final time. The anger and hurt he'd tamped down over the years rose and burned. He wanted her to know how much she'd hurt him. But at the same time, he didn't want to push her away again.

Lord, take away this burning inside me and give me the right words to say.

He felt no different, but something inside him propelled him out of the buggy and up the walk. He stopped just outside the threshold.

His *mutter* and Kathleen sat in the small sitting room. His *mutter* stood from an overstuffed rocker.

When the first word crossed his lips— *"Mutter"*—the bitterness washed away and love consumed him.

"My son. I've been praying for this moment every day." Her eyes glistened with tears.

Eyes that mirrored his. He'd forgotten he got most of his looks from her.

Staring at her, he realized he'd been wrong to stay away. Wrong to hold this bitterness in his heart. Wrong not to forgive her. She had suffered as much as he had. But he still wanted some answers and hoped she would tell him more than his *vater* had.

She motioned to the love seat Kathleen sat on.

"Please have a seat. I've made tea." She picked up a cup and handed it to him.

He took it and sat next to Kathleen, as it was the only available seat in the sitting room.

His *mutter* returned to her chair. "You must have a lot of questions for me."

"Too many. I scarcely know where to begin."

Kathleen inched forward and set her cup on the coffee table. "I'll leave the two of you to talk privately."

"Don't go." He had the urge to take her hand but didn't. She was supposed to be here.

"But I thought you two would like to speak freely."

Though his *mutter* looked as though she would like to be alone, she gave a nod. "You may stay."

He handed Kathleen her tea.

She took it and settled back in the seat.

His *mutter* spoke. "I can't tell you how happy I am that you've come."

"I should have come sooner."

"*Ne.* All in *Gott*'s timing. You probably want to know why I left. What has your *vater* told you?"

"He said he'd scarred your heart. That no matter what you told me that he loved me. And that…he still loves you."

"He does?"

"That's what he said. Why didn't you come back?" He glanced around the room. If he didn't know better, he would think he was in a *dawdy haus*. "You seem to live and dress as an Amish. Why live apart?"

"Your *vater* and I hurled bitter words at each other. I didn't come back because I didn't think your *vater* wanted me back."

"Why would you think that?"

"The last time I left, I told him if he wanted me back, he would have to come to me this time. He never came."

"I don't think he knows you're in town."

"He knows. Just as you knew."

His *vater* had seen her? Why hadn't he said anything?

"I was both hurt and proud of you for staying with him."

"How so?"

"Hurt, obviously, because you—my son— didn't choose to leave with me."

"I thought if *Vater* and I were both in one place, you'd come back to us. Why proud?"

"You chose the Amish way of life."

The English world held no appeal to him. "I know you and *Vater* fought, but was it so bad that you had to leave? I never saw him hit you or anything."

"It was his words that wounded. He blamed me that we couldn't have any more children."

"But you had me. You should have been able to have more."

"It's not that simple. But, I suppose, you deserve to know. Though your *vater* is your *vater* in every way that matters…he's not your biological *vater*."

Noah tried to make sense of her words. "I don't understand."

"When I went on *Rumspringa*, I was a foolish girl. In our community, everyone looked out for each other. And I never imagined someone hurting another. I believed what anyone told me. There was this English boy who was quite cute, and I liked it when he paid attention to me. He kept trying to get me to drink alcohol. I didn't like the taste and wouldn't. He gave me a cola instead. I started feeling dizzy. I don't remember much after that. Two months later, I realized I was pregnant. Your *vater* and I were already planning to marry. I told him about you. He said it didn't matter, that he would love you as his own as he would love all the children that came after you. He wanted a big family."

"But no more children came."

She shook her head. "He became more and more agitated about it. He said it was my sinful, wicked ways that denied him his own children.

He said he'd been wrong to marry me. I'd hoped he didn't mean it, that it was his own pain talking. All I know about your biological *vater* is that his first name was Justin."

No matter what your mutter tells you, know that I love you, son. This news didn't surprise him as much as he thought it should. He always knew he didn't resemble his *vater* and looked only partially like his *mutter*. "My *vater*'s name is Abraham. As you said, he is a *vater* in every way that matters." So his *vater* had been afraid of losing Noah and was hard on him to make sure his English blood didn't take him away. There was nothing to worry about. In no way did Noah feel English.

His *mutter* held her cup in her lap. "He must be very proud of you."

Noah thought back to the barn raising. His *vater* always wanted him to behave Amish so Noah wouldn't be tempted by the outside world. *Behave as an Amish should, and I'll be pleased enough.* "I think that maybe he is. Will you come back now?"

"If he wants me back. But I doubt he does."

"I'll talk to him."

After another hour and a half, Noah rose to leave. Kathleen stood up after him. He'd forgotten she was even there. Noah stepped forward and hugged his *mutter*. "Forgive me for staying away."

"Of course."

Too many years had been lost. "If *Vater* won't welcome you back, come live with me."

"In your *dawdy haus*?"

"Kathleen has her medical clinic in there, but my house has plenty of room for you."

"What about a wife and children?"

That pained him, thinking about what he'd lost and would never have. But his mind turned immediately to Kathleen at his side. "I don't have a wife or children. Not anymore."

His *mutter* patted his hand. "You will again one day."

Three months ago, he would have told her with certainly that he would never marry again. But now, he didn't know. He didn't plan to marry, but he wasn't as much opposed to it as he once was. "You are still welcome in my home." He stumbled over his next words but managed to get his sentence out fairly smoothly. "I have room." He'd almost said *we* have room. He and Kathleen weren't a *we*. Why would he think of them as such?

"I'll think about it. I don't want to foist myself upon your *vater* and make him uncomfortable."

"You wouldn't be. I'll come visit you again."

Noah needed to convince one of his parents to make the first move.

Noah waited until Sunday to approach his *vater*. He helped him unhitch his buggy. "She told me that another man is my biological *vater*."

His *vater* paused in unhooking the shaft from the harness. "I've always loved you as my own. I was hard on you because I wanted you to be a *gut* Amish and not go into the English world."

"I know you do. I think of no one else as my *vater* but you. You raised me, and you *are* my *vater*. And I *am* Amish." It surprised Noah how much he felt both of those things.

His *vater*'s eyes watered, and he gripped Noah's shoulders. "You have always made me… proud."

"If you go to her and ask her to come home, she will."

He released Noah. "She doesn't want me anymore. I've caused too much pain."

"*Ja*, she does. She's been waiting for you to ask her. When she left she told you—"

"That if I wanted her back, I would need to go to her."

"She said you have seen her in town. Why didn't you ever tell me?"

"At first, I was still angry with her. Then in

time, I was too ashamed of my actions. I didn't want you to think poorly of me."

If his *vater* didn't make an effort, Noah feared he would think poorly of him.

"I always pictured myself having a big family. Lots of children. When we didn't, I blamed your *mutter*."

"It wasn't her fault or yours. *Gott* determines the number of children families have."

"But it *is* my fault. I'm the reason we couldn't have more children. I've come to realize that the Lord blessed me with you because I couldn't have any others." His *vater* took a deep breath. "If I could do it all over, I'd treat her better."

"You can. You always encouraged me to be a *gut* Amish man. What would a *gut* Amish man do in this situation?" Though they both knew the answer, he spoke it aloud anyway. "Reconcile."

His *vater* didn't look convinced.

He could bring his parents' separation up to the other leaders and have Bishop Bontrager talk to him. If his *vater* refused to reconcile with his *mutter*, his *vater* would eventually be shunned. Noah couldn't do that to him. For now, he would let his parents find their own way back to each other.

Chapter Fourteen

❧

Decision Sunday had arrived, and Kathleen still didn't know what she was going to do. Her family congratulated her and Benjamin on finishing the classes to join church. She sat in church feeling like a hypocrite.

Again she pleaded, *Lord, what would You have me do?*

Stay or go? Both options seemed right in their own way. To stay would allow her to help her people as she'd always wanted to do, if they would allow her. If she left, she would have plenty of patients and respect as a doctor. If she stayed, she would be close to Noah. That thought made her smile. If she left, she could have everything—a respected medical practice, a husband and children. Ethan would expect her to marry him. Could she be happy with him?

Standing up front, the bishop gave his oration

about the importance of church membership and called those forward who wished to complete the process to become church members.

Noah stared hard at her as though willing her to stand.

Noah's *mutter*, Heddy Lambright, sat with her husband. She seemed to have come back. Hopefully for *gut*.

All Kathleen had wanted was to be a respected doctor in her community. There was nothing wrong in that. Then a realization struck her as hard as if someone had slapped her.

Gott had not called her to be *respected*. Just a doctor for her people, in whatever form that took. For all those years away in school and hospitals, if she saved just one life—which she'd done—then that was how it was to be. Was everything she'd worked for just to have the medicine on hand to save her nephew's life?

She glanced around the room. These were her people, and she would serve them in whatever manner *Gott* saw fit. She was a doctor. A very *gut* doctor. But that wasn't what defined her. She was Amish. That too didn't define her. Being a child of *Gott*, *that* was what defined her. She would obey His calling on her life.

As she stood, Noah released his breath. This would make him happy, which pleased her.

Ethan would need to be told of her final decision. He wouldn't be pleased, but she had to follow her heart. And her heart belonged to *Gott*. *Gott* wanted her here in her community.

When the membership ceremony was completed, Kathleen felt a stifling weight lift from her. She hadn't realized that the burden of not being a member of church had weighed so heavily on her. She was finally fully Amish. Now maybe the church leaders would see that she was serious about her commitment and start accepting her as their resident doctor.

Kathleen walked out of the Zooks' home into the warm fall day. She had definitely made the right decision. *Gott*'s peace had enveloped her. The sun seemed brighter and the sky clearer. Though she'd committed herself to this community for the rest of her life, bound by the rules of the *Ordnung*, she felt somehow freer.

Noah strolled up next to her. Along with him came his familiar scent of wood and honey. "The leadership is pleased you decided to join."

"I'm pleased as well."

"You seem happier than you did before the service."

She smiled. "I am."

"Had something been concerning you?"

She didn't know if she should tell him. But she took a deep breath and spoke. "When I arrived this morning, I hadn't decided if I was going to stay and join or not."

He pulled his head back as though surprised. "Really? You don't regret your decision, do you?"

"*Ne*, of course not."

"What helped make up your mind? Because there are still certain members of the leadership who haven't changed their opinions about your being a doctor."

"I thought I wanted respect as a doctor from our people. If I couldn't get it from them, then I thought maybe I was supposed to seek it elsewhere."

"And now?"

"I was looking in the wrong places. I realized I needed to be seeking approval from *Gott* and only *Gott*."

"And are you?"

"*Ja.*"

"Even if you aren't granted continuing permission to be a doctor here?"

"*Ja.* But will you promise me something?"

"If I can."

"If you think I'm seeking approval from anyone but *Gott*, would you tell me? I don't want to become misguided again." That was a lot to ask of someone who wasn't a family member. But she sensed she could trust him to be honest with her. And she wanted to confide in him. She felt as close to him as her family. And he lived nearby. And she would see him often with her clinic on his property.

"I'm honored you would ask such a thing of me. I'll do my best."

"Danki."

"I suppose we should see if there is any food left."

With a chuckle, she headed toward the tables. "Amish women *always* prepare more food than what could ever be eaten."

He chuckled too. "Then let's get food before all the *gut* stuff is gone."

She turned a withering look on him. "*Gut* stuff? What here will not be *gut*?"

He heaved a deep breath. "Let me say it this way. Will you join me for lunch?"

Oh. She should say *ne*. If she agreed, he might take it as permission to court her. Courting, marriage, family were still sadly not an option. She shouldn't encourage him, but she said, *"Ja."*

As she reached the buffet line, she noticed Preacher Hochstetler.

Though he stood in line, his eyes were closed, his face red and his breathing strained and fast.

Kathleen left Noah and maneuvered around

several people. "Preacher Hochstetler, are you feeling all right?"

His eyes opened, and he scowled at her. "I'm fine. Leave me alone." Sweat beaded on his upper lip. Even on this warm fall day, he shouldn't be sweating with zero exertion.

She took his arm. "Come sit down."

He pulled free. "Don't touch me. I don't need your meddling ways."

Noah had caught up to her. "Paul, you don't look well."

His wife, Elizabeth, spoke up. "That's what I've been telling him all morning, but he won't listen to me."

Just then, he set his plate on the edge of the buffet table and rubbed his left arm. "I'm fine, I tell all of you."

He was *not* fine. If he wasn't already having a heart attack, he soon would.

Kathleen turned to Noah. "Call 911."

"What? Why?"

Staring at him, she willed him to understand. He mouthed, "Heart attack?"

She nodded.

He turned to someone else and whispered in his ear. That person ran off.

Kathleen glanced around and saw her youngest brother close by, probably back for seconds. "Get my medical pack out of the buggy."

Samuel nodded and walked off.

"Run!"

He leapt into a run.

Kathleen focused her attention back on Preacher Hochstetler.

He wadded up his hand and pressed it to his chest. "Don't touch me," he ground out between clenched teeth.

Kathleen stepped toward him. "You're likely having a heart attack. Let me help."

He shook his head.

Just as she was about to grip his arm, Noah grasped hers and held her back.

She jerked her head around. "What are you doing?"

"The leadership was clear that you weren't allowed to give medical treatment to anyone who didn't want it or to their family members."

She shifted her gaze from Noah to the ailing preacher and back. "He's going to die. Shun me if you want."

Thankfully, he released her.

By now, those closest to them had backed away, and those who had been seated, eating or milling around had closed in to form a dense, wide circle.

As Kathleen took hold of the preacher's arm, he dropped to his knees. She went down with him.

He grasped her arm and opened his mouth,

but no words came out. He stared hard at her with glassy eyes.

"Don't worry. You're going to be all right." Even if he didn't make it, that statement was true, because he would be in heaven with the Lord. She glanced around the crowd. Where was Samuel with her medical kit? "Did someone call for an ambulance?"

Noah answered. "I sent Jacob."

Samuel called from the back of the crowd. "I can't get through!"

"Let him through!" Kathleen yelled.

The crowd shuffled enough to let her brother pass. He dropped the bag next to her.

"Help me lay him on his back."

Noah did.

"Roll up his sleeve as far as you can get it."

Noah complied.

Kathleen wrenched the zipper on the pack open and yanked supplies out and dropped them in the grass. She pulled out a pair of latex-free surgical gloves and put them on. She set her stethoscope in her lap. Seizing her blood pressure cuff, she jerked that free. She wrapped it around Preacher Hochstetler's arm and pumped it up. She jammed the earpieces of her stethoscope into place and put the round end in the inside crook of his arm. She slowly released the air pressure.

Two-ten over one-oh-five.

Panic rose in her. The preacher would die for sure.

His face was red. His eyes were closed. No detectable rise or fall of his chest.

She reached for the preacher's shirt buttons.

Noah gripped her hands. "What are you doing?"

"Trying to save his life."

"But you can't undo his shirt."

"I'm a doctor." True, it was very inappropriate for an Amish woman to half undress an Amish man, but this was an emergency. "*You* unbutton his shirt while I get the AED."

He released her hand and went to work on the shirt. "What's an AED?"

"A portable defibrillator. I can restart his heart with it."

He nodded as he finished unbuttoning the shirt. "Everyone turn around. And pray."

The crowd shifted as one until all backs faced the inside of the circle.

How had she ever become a doctor when she'd come from such a reserved upbringing? She'd been forced to get over her discomfort fast.

She pulled out the red-and-yellow AED case, then opened the lid and removed the package with the defibrillator pads.

The AED spoke, "Begin by removing all clothing from the patient's chest. Tear open package and remove pads."

She did so and untangled the attached cords.

"Peel one pad from plastic liner. Place one pad on bare upper chest," the mechanical machine's voice instructed.

She peeled the pad and reached to stick it to the preacher's chest.

Noah stopped her. "It would be better if I do it. Tell me what to do." He took the pad.

"Place one pad on bare upper chest," the machine repeated.

She pointed. "Put it there and press it down firmly."

He followed her instructions.

"Remove second pad and place second pad on bare lower chest," the machine instructed.

Kathleen pointed again. "Press it down firmly. It needs to have *gut* adhesion."

He did so.

"Now take your hands away so the machine can read his signs." Kathleen held her hands up.

"Do not touch patient," the machine said.

Noah pulled his hands back.

Kathleen spoke to the crowd. "Stand clear everyone. Don't touch him." That was a foolish thing to say. Everyone was several feet away. And all but the leaders had their backs turned.

The machine spoke again. "Analyzing rhythm. Do not touch the patient. Analyzing rhythm. Shock advised. Charging. Stand clear. Press flashing button to deliver shock."

"Clear! Don't touch him!" Kathleen pressed the flashing red heart-shaped button. She prayed this worked.

The preacher's body jerked.

"Shock delivered," the machine announced. "It is now safe to touch the patient. Give thirty compressions then two breaths."

Kathleen clasped one hand over the other and pressed on the preacher's chest.

Noah held out his hands. "Let me do that. It's not right for you to be touching him in that manner."

She gave him a withering glance and continued.

He'd done his due diligence in asking.

Kathleen inclined her head toward the AED. "There's a mouth barrier mask in the kit. Take it out and extend it."

He did.

"When I tell you to, place it over his mouth and nose and give him two breaths. Now." She pulled her hands away.

After two minutes of this back-and-forth between compressions and breaths, the machine spoke. "Do not touch patient. Reanalyzing."

Kathleen took her hands away.

"Shock advised."

"Clear!" *Please, Lord, make this work.* She pressed the button, and the preacher's body jerked again. She resumed the chest compressions.

After another two minutes, the AED did not advise another shock, and Preacher Hochstetler blinked his eyes.

He was alive.

She drew in a relieved breath and patted his shoulder. "Lie still. An ambulance is on its way." She monitored his vitals and wrote down his blood pressure every few minutes on the palm of her rubber glove.

This was why she had become a doctor. This was why she wanted to stay in her community to be a doctor. This was why she'd made the right decision to stay.

Soon sirens wailed in the distance.

"Everyone move back so the paramedics can get to him," Kathleen said.

Noah stood and made sure the people cleared a path.

When the paramedics rushed over, Kathleen gave them Preacher Hochstetler's pertinent information and all that had been done to help him.

One of the paramedics stared at her. "Even

though you look like one, you don't talk or act like any Amish I've ever met."

She would likely always be part English in her Amish body, clothes and world. But that was finally all right with her. "I'm a doctor."

Soon the preacher was secured on a gurney and put into the back of the ambulance. Elizabeth Hochstetler climbed in as well.

Kathleen stared at her hands. They shook from the aftereffects of the adrenaline rush. She hoped no one noticed, or they wouldn't trust her.

Noah stood next to Kathleen as several people congratulated her. He couldn't believe what she had done. "You saved his life."

"I need to go to the hospital."

He nodded. "I'll take you."

She knelt down and crammed her supplies back into her medical kit.

"You could have easily obeyed the leadership's decision and done nothing. Then your main opposition would no longer be a problem, and you would not be blamed."

"I couldn't do that."

"I know. That's why I released you. Let's go." Noah drove his larger, covered buggy. He was glad he'd opted for this vehicle instead of the smaller open one. With the cooler fall evenings, he hadn't wanted Kathleen to get cold if she agreed to a buggy ride later. But this wasn't exactly what he'd had in mind.

"Could you drive faster?"

"The *Ordnung* is specific about the speed at which we are permitted to drive."

"We can have solar panels for electricity and telephones, but in an emergency, we can travel no faster than a fast trot."

"If this truly were an emergency, it would be permissible to run the horse. But it's not."

"Not an emergency? Preacher Hochstetler went into cardiac arrest. If that's not an emergency, then what is?"

"He was taken by ambulance and is receiving medical treatment. He's getting the best care he can. Whether the horse runs, trots, or walks, there is nothing more *you* can do at the moment."

She let out a quick breath. "I know. You're right. I just want to be there in case they have any questions, and so I can know what's going on."

"Ah. So that's it. You don't like not knowing something."

She huffed out a single laugh. "I guess not. *Danki* for driving me."

"Of course."

Once at the hospital, Kathleen dismissed him.

"You don't have to stay. I'll get in touch with my parents to get a ride home."

"I'm staying. I might not have to, but I am."

Tears filled her eyes. "*Danki*. I can't tell you how much your being here means to me."

He'd hoped she would appreciate his presence. He didn't want to be anywhere else except at her side. He'd seen her hands shaking. "I'm happy to stay. Just let me know what you need. I'll help in whatever way I can." He parked the buggy in the designated buggy parking area.

Kathleen rushed to Elizabeth Hochstetler's side. "Have you heard any news?"

Elizabeth gripped her hand. "They say he's stable. They said he is only alive because you used that machine on him. *Danki* for saving his life."

"*Ne*, I'm just a person. It was *Gott*. Without Him, nothing I did would have been enough."

The woman hugged Kathleen. "*Danki* for listening to *Gott* rather than man. Your obedience has given me back my husband."

Kathleen opened her mouth again, most likely to protest who should get the credit.

But Noah touched her arm to stop her. "Let's sit."

Soon the waiting room filled with their Amish brothers and sisters. People huddled in the center of the room, round after round of people, praying. This was the heart of the Amish. Coming together to help others in need. Noah was proud to be Amish and among such faithful people.

And to be here for Kathleen.

Chapter Fifteen

The next morning, Kathleen sat at her desk in her clinic and called the hospital to check on Preacher Hochstetler.

"I'm sorry. I can't give you any information on him. HIPAA, you know."

Ja, Kathleen knew. She was just hoping the nurse would give her a little information because she'd been the first attending physician. She didn't want to get the nurse in trouble by pressing the matter. "Thanks anyway."

She pressed the end button and stared at the phone. She had another call to make. Though it had to be done, she didn't relish it. Putting it off wouldn't make it any easier. Maybe she could simply "forget" and never make the call.

That wouldn't work. Besides being rude and breaking a promise, Ethan would likely show up here at some point soon and ask for her decision. She'd told him she would be making it around this time.

She removed his business card from her top desk drawer. She flipped it over to stare at the handwritten cell number on the back. Maybe she could call his office and leave a message. *Ne.* That would be rude as well.

If she could defy her Amish leaders by going to college, medical school, becoming a doctor and returning to be a doctor for them when they didn't want her to be, she could make a simple phone call.

She took a deep breath and punched in the number.

It rang several times with no answer.

Maybe he was in surgery.

That would be perfect. She could leave a message on his personal phone and not have to talk to him.

"This better be important." His gruff voice sounded tired.

No hello or pleasantries.

"Ethan? Is that you?"

"Who—Kathleen?"

"Ja."

His voice brightened. "Kathleen. I'm so glad you called."

"Ne, you're not. I woke you up again, didn't I?"

"I just got off a double. I might not have been glad to be woken up, but I *am* glad you called."

He wouldn't be when she told him.

"I'm sorry for waking you. You should turn your phone off when you're sleeping."

"I do, but I have it programmed to let two numbers through. The hospital and your clinic. I didn't look at the caller ID. Thought it was my office."

Ugh. This wasn't going to be *gut*. He was going to be disappointed. She wanted to ask him how the children's clinic was progressing, but small talk would not be fitting. "You told me to let you know when I came to a decision."

"Stop right there. I can hear the hesitancy in your voice. You're not going to tell me good news, are you?"

"I'm sorry."

"Don't say that. You should see the kids. They need you so much. I met this little boy Nicky last week. He has a cleft palate. We could help him."

"You'll have to help him on your own. I'm needed here."

"You're needed *here* too. The *clinic* needs you. The *children* need you." His voice dropped. "*I* need you."

He was once again offering her everything. But instead of being tempted as she had been before, it made her feel sad. Sad for him. "I'm where I'm supposed to be. I saved a man's life yesterday." She left out *Gott*'s part in all of it because Ethan wouldn't understand. And maybe that was it. Ethan didn't need *Gott*. He was an excellent doctor and believed he'd become one all on his own with no help from anyone, let alone an invisible *Gott* he didn't believe in. She felt sad for him in a different, deeper way. She would pray more fervently for him.

"You could save lives here too."

"That would be true anywhere I went. You're meant to do great things as a doctor. I'm meant to be here. Just being a doctor for my community is a big thing. I wish you all the best."

"Don't say that. It sounds so final."

"This is final, Ethan. I've made my decision."

He hung up without another word or argument.

She had done the right thing. Ethan had a different path. One that didn't include her. Her path was here. And she had no regrets about that.

With no appointments scheduled and nothing to keep her at the clinic, she headed back home to help her *mutter* and sisters harvest the garden and start some canning.

Later in the morning, Kathleen opened the front door of her parents' home for Bishop Bontrager. *"Hallo."* She ushered him into the living room where *Mum* and *Dat* were. "Have you heard any word on Preacher Hochstetler?"

Nodding, the bishop sat. "He is doing well because of you."

She corrected him. "Because of *Gott*. My efforts would go only as far as *Gott* would allow them to."

"Kathleen," *Dat* admonished.

"It's all right." The bishop's smile widened. "*Gott*'s part is a given. But don't minimize what you did. No one else had the training, knowledge and equipment."

This bishop was so different from the hard man he'd been when she'd left.

"I want to visit him at the hospital."

"I think it's best to wait until he comes home."

She didn't want to wait. She was his doctor. *Ne*. She wasn't. And never would be. He likely wouldn't let her anywhere near him or permit her to help him or anyone else in the community.

"Now—" the bishop inclined his head "—if you'll allow me to speak with your parents."

"Of course. I'll get some refreshments." Kathleen left for the kitchen. She quickly filled a plate with old-time cinnamon jumbo cookies and poured three cups of coffee.

When she returned to the living room, both her parents were beaming.

Kathleen set the tray on the coffee table, handed a cup to each of them and offered cookies all around.

Dat caught her gaze. "Would you find Ruby and tell her to come in here?"

A visit from Bishop Bontrager in the fall, asking to speak to the parents of a young woman who had a serious beau could mean only one thing. A proposal! "I'll get her." Kathleen hurried outside to where she'd last seen Ruby in the garden. The English thought the Amish way of delivering a proposal offer through the bishop was a bit odd, but it had its own sense that one couldn't fully appreciate when one wasn't raised Amish.

She found she was a little jealous of Ruby. She would marry, be a wife and *mutter*. Things Kathleen would never do or be. She steeled herself to be who *Gott* had called her to be. A doctor. *Gott* had already demonstrated that this was what He wanted for her life. And she was grateful to be back with her Amish people and determined to be content with that.

She got to the garden and called, "Ruby?"

"At the end by the pumpkins," came her sister's voice from beyond the green leaves, vegetation and foliage.

Kathleen hurried along and jumped over a row of carrots.

Ruby held her apron up filled with red ripe tomatoes and pea pods. "What's got you in a rush?"

"You have to come to the house."

"Let me finish picking tomatoes from this plant."

In both of her hands, Kathleen took her sister's free hand, the one that wasn't holding up her apron. "You have to come right away. No time to dally."

Ruby straightened. "You asked me to tell you when you were acting too English. Now is one of those times. There is nothing to rush so much about."

"There is today. Bishop Bontrager is at the house. He's waiting for you. You know what that means."

Ruby's eyes widened, and she bit her bottom lip. "I knew Jonathan was anxious for us to marry, but I never expected him to ask for me the very first day he could."

Kathleen hugged her sister. "I'm so happy for you."

"You'll deliver all my babies, won't you?"

"Of course. I'd be honored." A feeling of loss flowed through Kathleen. Loss for things she would never have. She thought of Noah.

"Your turn will be next. I just know it."

Kathleen knew differently. Yesterday had

been confirmation from *Gott* that she was right—or rather *Gott* was right—about where she was supposed to be. Here in the Amish world, being a doctor for her people. Most of them might not understand her decision to remain single and be a doctor rather than marry and have children. Might not understand her call from *Gott*. But she did, and that was what mattered.

But she wouldn't ruin her sister's day with her gloomy thoughts for herself. She'd made her choice all those years ago, and was honored to have been given such a calling by *Gott*. His ways were higher than her ways, His thoughts higher than hers. How could helping to save a life compare to selfishly wanting a husband—Noah—and children?

Later that same afternoon, Kathleen opened the door once again for Bishop Bontrager. "You're back. What a nice surprise. Come in."

The bishop had a strange expression. "Are your parents here?"

"*Ja.* Is something wrong? Preacher Hochstetler didn't take a turn for the worse, did he?" She knew she should have gone to the hospital.

"Relax. Paul is fine. This is a completely different matter."

She was glad to know the preacher was fine.

"I'll go find them." She went to the kitchen and retrieved a cup of coffee and another plate of cookies, and brought them back to the bishop. "For you, while you wait."

She went out to the garden, where her *mum* and sisters picked vegetables to can. *"Mum?"*

Her *mutter*'s head popped up from behind a row of climbing pea vines. "What is it?"

Kathleen picked her way over, making sure not to step on any plants or vegetables. "Bishop Bontrager is back. He wants to talk to you and *Dat.*"

Mum furrowed her eyebrows. "He is? We weren't expecting him again."

Ruby hurried over. "It's not Jonathan, do you think? He didn't change his mind, did he? I hope nothing happened to him."

Mum turned to Ruby. "You better come with me." *Mum* turned back to Kathleen. "Can you find your *dat*?"

Kathleen nodded. She'd planned to and took off toward the barn as *Mum* and Ruby headed for the house. She found *Dat*, and they headed to the house as well. As they entered through the kitchen, Ruby sauntered from the living room with a smile. "Told you so." She continued out to the garden.

Kathleen turned to *Dat*. "What was that about?"

"I'll go find out," *Dat* headed into the living room.

"I'll bring you and *Mum* coffee."

She prepared cups of coffee and carried them into the living room. The trio abruptly stopped talking. Obviously, the topic wasn't for her. She handed *Dat* and *Mum* their cups. "Is there anything else I can get?"

Mum shook her head.

Dat motioned to the open spot on the couch next to *Mum*. "Have a seat, Kathleen."

She gave him a quizzical look. This couldn't be *gut*. If the bishop was here for her, she was likely to be shunned for her actions yesterday when Preacher Hochstetler went into cardiac arrest. She was not sorry for allowing *Gott* to use her to save his life. She straightened. She would take whatever punishment the leaders saw fit.

Bishop Bontrager cleared his throat. "Had I known about this earlier, I would have conducted this business then. Now you all will just think I came for more of these cookies." He chuckled.

Why was he making light of the situation? This was obviously a serious matter for him to return so soon and not put it off for another day. "Am I to be shunned?"

The bishop's eyes widened. "Is that what you think? The leaders haven't met on the events that transpired yesterday. *Ne*, I'm here on another matter. There has been an offer of marriage for you."

"What?" Kathleen stared. Who would want to marry her?

The bishop chuckled again. "Apparently you weren't expecting an offer. Interesting."

"Who would offer for me? I've gone against so many points of the *Ordnung*, no man would want a wife like me. And most know that I never plan to marry. I wouldn't make any man a *gut* wife."

"Well, obviously Noah Lambright thinks you would."

Her heart leapt for joy, and then was dashed into pieces. "Noah?" This couldn't be right. Noah also never planned to marry. Losing his wife had been too painful.

"*Ja*. Noah. What shall I tell him?"

Why would Noah offer for her? Part of her wanted to say *ja*. If she were ever to marry, Noah would be whom she would choose. But she couldn't marry. Hadn't *Gott* made that clear? She was to be a doctor. Not a wife and *mutter*. That made her heart ache. She wanted to be all three. "Tell him I'm very honored by his offer, but I can't marry him."

Mum gasped. "Kathleen. Why would you

turn him down? He's a *gut* man and will make you a wonderful husband."

She knew that, and he already fit so well into their family. "*Gott* called me to be a doctor. Not a wife." Tears pricked her eyes. "I need to obey Him."

The bishop studied her a moment before he spoke. "I think you should reconsider. I'll give you time to think about your decision."

"I don't need time. I've made my decision. I can't marry Noah." The words choked out. "Tell him my answer is *ne*." A chasm of pain opened up inside her, and she shot to her feet and ran upstairs.

She stood by the window. How could he have offered for her when he knew she would say *ne*? She recalled his warm lips on hers. All those years ago, when she'd decided to become a doctor, had she known it would be Noah she couldn't marry, she might not have had the strength of will to become a doctor.

Then a terrible thought occurred to her. What if the bishop and other leaders had successfully pressured Noah into this? He'd said he wouldn't court anyone if they asked, but maybe he hadn't had a choice. If she had a husband, she would have to obey him. And if he said she couldn't be a doctor, she would be honor bound to obey. But she'd already committed to *Gott* to be a doctor. She couldn't go against Him. *Ne.* Sadly, she couldn't marry Noah.

Noah stood in his yard when Bishop Bontrager's buggy pulled up. This was it. The bishop would have an answer from Kathleen. He'd wanted to talk to her directly and was going to after the service yesterday, but then Paul Hochstetler'd had a heart attack and nothing else mattered. He wanted to talk to her directly so he could tell her so much more than what she'd hear from the bishop. But this way was probably better, because she would know he was serious. That his offer was genuine.

Bishop Bontrager pulled his buggy to a stop and got out. "*Hallo*, Noah."

Why did the bishop seem reserved? And why wasn't he smiling? "Has something happened in the community?" Maybe he hadn't had a chance to talk to Kathleen and her parents yet.

The bishop shook his head. "It's Kathleen Yoder."

His gut wrenched. "Is she all right?"

"*Ja.* But I'm sorry to say that she turned down your offer of marriage."

His heart dropped to his shoes. "Turned me down?"

"I'm afraid so. Said she can't be both a doc-

tor and a wife. She said she will never marry.
I'm so sorry."

What was he going to do now? "*Danki*,
Bishop." Should he try to persuade her? Should
he move to the far side of the community so he
would only have to see her every other Sunday?
The one consolation was that he wouldn't have
to see her married to another man.

Unless…she fell in love and changed her
mind.

He'd never considered that she would turn
him down. In his mind, he'd pictured her de-
lighted. She would have thrown her arms
around him in a fit of overwhelming joy, then
have to control herself. Then one day, he could
tell their children how English their *mutter* was.
She obviously didn't care as much for him as
he'd thought and hoped.

He had never planned to marry again after
Rachel died. After about six months, people
started encouraging him to marry again. It
hadn't seemed right so soon. Then he just wasn't
interested. Then he felt *Gott* calling him to remain single, which suited him fine. He had been
enjoying his single life with only a small niggling every once in a while that he should contribute to the continuation of the Amish people
and their Amish way of life. But those moments
were brief and passed quickly. And they came

more and more seldom. *Gott* had called him to a different life than his Amish brothers and sisters. Being alone had become a comfortable habit. He had been content. And happy.

Until…

Until Kathleen returned and turned his contentment into longing and his happiness into dissatisfaction. He wanted more. It had been as though he'd been waiting for more than contentment. Though he hadn't known he'd been waiting, he realized he had.

When Kathleen showed up, walking along the roadside, his heart came back to life. As though he'd been waiting for *her*. Everything he'd done for the past three years was in preparation for her. He could see that now.

So if he'd been preparing for her return, why didn't she feel the same way about him? It made no sense. Why would *Gott* do that to him? Why get Noah's hopes up just to dash them? Too many questions and no answers.

Well, one answer.

Ne.

Chapter Sixteen

On Friday, Preacher Hochstetler was released from the hospital.

Bishop Bontrager sent word that Kathleen's presence was required at the preacher's home. *Dat* insisted on driving her even though she told him she would be fine going by herself.

"If my daughter is going to be summoned by the bishop after…after all that has happened— and I'm including the time you were away— then I'm going to be there."

"Me too." *Mum* put on her coat.

Kathleen didn't need a babysitter, let alone two. Now that the preacher was home, the bishop and Preacher Hochstetler probably wanted to chastise her for going against the preacher's wishes. Helping him when she was told in no uncertain terms not to touch him. They would likely shun her for her disobedience now that she was a member. But she didn't mind. Elizabeth Hochstetler had her husband and her children still had their *vater*. She would never be sorry for that. This visit would give her a chance to check on him.

Even if Preacher Hochstetler would never welcome her medical expertise, others in the community had to see how vital her presence as a doctor was. Whether approved or not, others would seek her out. Even if they didn't, they would feel more reassured having her near, knowing she would be there if needed. They had seen it with Isaac being stabbed with that stick in his thigh. Though she hadn't been allowed to physically tend to the boy, he was doing well and his wound had healed. He still had a slight limp but was running around again.

Then, she hadn't been allowed to aid her nephew Mark. But because she was there with her medical supplies, he had been treated and was alive today. Bless little Nancy for stepping in where the adults were stymied by rules and tradition. What a blessing that Nancy didn't have to watch her younger sibling die as Kathleen and Gloria had so many years ago.

And then there was the preacher. She had been able to be the one to administer medical treatment to him.

But she hadn't done any of those things to get

her community to accept her as a doctor. She had done them because she wanted to help her people. So she would hold her head high regardless of what Preacher Hochstetler, the bishop or any of the leaders had to say.

Deacon Zook came out of the house when *Dat* pulled to a stop.

What was he doing here? She saw several buggies. Were all the church leaders here? If so, this meeting was definitely to shun her. She'd hoped to check on how Preacher Hochstetler was doing. But that wouldn't be likely now.

She took a deep breath and got out of the buggy.

Deacon Zook smiled.

Why? Was he trying to confuse her? Trying to lower her defenses?

She squared her shoulders and smiled back. *"Guten Morgen."*

"Guten Morgen. Please come inside. Everyone is waiting for you."

Everyone. That wasn't daunting.

Preacher Hochstetler's oldest son, Eli, walked the horse and buggy away.

Dat flanked Kathleen on one side and *Mum* on the other. Kathleen was grateful for their support and glad they had insisted on coming.

Mum leaned closer and whispered. "We are very proud of you."

Dat nodded. "Very proud."

Her parents were proud of her, even after disobeying the leaders and being away so long? That meant more to her than any number of patients. Their pleasure in her was magnified by the pleasure she sensed from *Gott*. Like a confirmation. *Well done, my gut and faithful servant. Gott*'s words from the book of Matthew ministered to her like a salve on a burn, cooling and comforting.

Inside, Preacher Hochstetler sat in the living room with all the other leaders, including Noah, as Kathleen had suspected. Noah didn't look directly at her. Not after her turning down his offer of marriage. So now she would have at least two church leadership members openly against her. Noah's opposition hurt worse.

She would be respectful but would refuse to stop practicing medicine. If she had to spend the rest of her life in the community as a shunned member, she would. And she would help any of them every chance she got.

The preacher's wife crossed to Kathleen. "I just want to say—"

Preacher Hochstetler spoke abruptly. "Sit down, woman, and let us conduct our business first."

Elizabeth Hochstetler squeezed Kathleen's hand and mouthed with a smile, *"Danki."*

Kathleen gave her a nod, then turned to Preacher Hochstetler. "You shouldn't excite yourself. You need rest so your heart can heal."

He waved his hand back and forth in front of him. "*Ja, ja.* The doctors at the hospital told me all that. We have important matters to take care of."

"But you will do as they advised?"

"*Ja.* Now have a seat."

All the leaders were standing except Preacher Hochstetler.

She didn't want to be the only other one in the room sitting. "I'll stand, *danki.*"

He narrowed his eyes at her. "You are a stubborn one."

Rather than taking his comment as an insult, she would look at it as a compliment. *"Danki."*

He widened his eyes at that and raised one eyebrow. "About the matter of you running a medical clinic and helping people—who, by the way, expressly told you not to."

"I regret nothing I've done." She wouldn't add that without her, he wouldn't be here to criticize her actions.

"I'm sure you don't. The bishop has allowed me to be the one to tell you the outcome of our vote on these matters."

She braced herself, and her anger rose even before he started speaking.

"First the matter of your clinic. You have permission to run your clinic for the *gut* of the community."

"But… What?"

He chuckled. Preacher Hochstetler actually chuckled. Had she ever seen him do that?

"The vote was unanimous. We believe your clinic will help the community tremendously."

Unanimous? She looked around the room at each member of the leadership. Each returned her gaze with a nod. She let her gaze linger on Noah. He too gave her a nod, then averted his gaze. She couldn't believe they all voted for her to continue her clinic. "How long of a trial period am I allowed?"

"No more trial period. The clinic is in the best interest of everyone. There are other communities who bring in an *Englisher* doctor. We have no need for that. As to your disobedience in going to college and becoming a doctor, we decided since you hadn't joined church, you weren't breaking any rules. But don't let that become common knowledge to others. We still disapprove of higher education because it takes our young people out of the community for so long, and we will discourage anyone who tries to do as you did. But what's done is done."

This was what she wanted from the start. To be accepted in her community as a doctor. And now that the church leaders had declared her clinic admissible, her fellow Amish brothers and sisters wouldn't hesitate to come and allow her to treat them.

"On the matter of helping someone, or their family, who have expressly told you not to, you *must* refrain. If someone, or their family member, dies because they refuse your medical treatment, then their blood is *not* on your hands."

This, she might not be able to abide by. If she saw a life-threatening situation, how could she not step in? She would have to pray about that one and see how the Lord directed her.

"As for me and my family, you have my permission to treat us as you see fit. And I won't intervene in your assistance with any community member." He held out his hand to her.

She stepped forward and took it. She wasn't sure why he was offering his hand nor why she took it.

He squeezed her hand. "*Danki* for being stubborn and saving my life."

Kathleen stared. She never expected gratitude. "*Bitte*. But it was *Gott* who actually saved your life. I did what I could and the rest was up to Him."

"*Danki* for allowing Him to use you."

"*Bitte*."

She couldn't believe this turn of events. She

looked to Noah, who stared at the ground. Had he given up his chance to marry her by voting in favor of her clinic?

As soon as the business at hand was completed at Preacher Hochstetler's, Noah backed out of the room and stepped into the kitchen. He'd positioned himself to be able to escape without notice. The oldest Hochstetler daughter, a willowy twelve-year-old, blinked at him as he passed through the room. He gave her a smile and a nod before exiting.

He hurried to the corral where he'd left his coat hanging over the railing. He swung it on.

From behind him came Kathleen's voice. *"Danki."*

He turned but didn't meet her gaze. Why had she broken his heart? "For what?"

"For voting in favor of my clinic."

"We need a doctor. It was the right thing to do." He hurried into the corral and walked out his horse.

"I didn't expect you to vote in my favor."

He swung up onto his horse's bare back. "The clinic is right for the community."

Though true, he'd also wanted to give Kathleen what she wanted. Even if that didn't include him.

Why couldn't Kathleen accept his offer of

marriage? Hadn't he always supported her efforts? Why couldn't she see she could be both a doctor *and* a wife? Maybe she just didn't care for him enough. Maybe she didn't care for him as much as he did her.

He would need to pray to figure out what the Lord wanted of him. He'd thought he knew, hence the reason for offering for Kathleen. Now he didn't know what his next steps were.

Kathleen stared up at Noah on his horse. She hadn't been to the clinic at all this past week after refusing his offer of marriage. And he, in turn, hadn't been to a single meal at their home. He had been avoiding her. Well, hadn't she been avoiding him first by not going to the clinic all week? She didn't know what to say. Anything she could think of would likely make matters worse. But she didn't want him to leave like this.

If they were going to be neighbors and in the same community for the rest of their lives, they were going to need to find a way to coexist.

The cold fall air seeped through her clothes and bit her skin. She didn't care.

She wrapped her arms around herself. "Noah? I need to know something."

He didn't dismount. "What?"

"Why did you offer for me?"

His voice came out flat. "The same reason

any man offers for a woman. Because he wants to marry her."

She rubbed her hands vigorously on her upper arms. "Was your offer a ploy to keep me from being a doctor?"

He stared hard down at her. "Is that really what you thought?"

She had hurt and insulted him. "I didn't want to."

"But you did."

"You said you'd never marry again."

"Sometimes things change."

"I want to hear from you that you weren't trying to manipulate me. That the other leaders didn't pressure you into it."

"You think someone put me up to offering for you?"

She continued to rub her arms. "You made it very clear when we first met that you weren't looking for another wife, ever, and wouldn't marry again. You were going to remain single."

He climbed down. "That was how I felt when we first met. Most of the eligible Amish women knew that about me, though some chose to ignore it. You being new—or at least not knowing—I didn't want you to get any ideas." He took off his coat and wrapped it around her.

His warmth enveloped her.

He continued. "Little did I know that you

had the same outlook. You didn't want to get married either. It made you easy to talk to and be around, without feeling like there had to be something more. But then things changed. I guess I misjudged what we had. My mistake."

"What we had? I thought it was friendship. Wasn't it?"

"It started out that way, but it changed along the way. I saw life differently. I saw *my* life differently. Instead of a solitary life, I saw you in it with me."

She'd had no idea. She'd had to keep reining in her own heart because she knew he wouldn't marry and she couldn't. Maybe that was why she was so adamant about not marrying because she knew there was no chance that he would offer for her. "So you truly do care for me?"

"Care? What I feel is so much more than care. I love you. That's why I offered for you."

"Oh, Noah. I love you too."

"Could have fooled me. You said *ne*. You thought I was coerced by the other leaders. You thought I'd stoop that low." His expression changed from hurt to expectation. "Now that you know I wasn't compelled by anyone or anything but my heart, will you reconsider my offer?"

"What about my being a doctor? I can't exactly marry and do that too."

He took both of her hands in his. "Your drive and determination are only two of the reasons I fell in love with you. We'll work out the doctor thing. If you marry me, you'll be a lot closer to your clinic. Jessica reminded me that several married women—women with children—run fruit and vegetable stands and make quilts and more."

"You would let me continue to be a doctor?"

"Provided the leaders are agreeable. If they aren't, we might be shunned."

We? He would stand with her? "You would risk shunning for me?"

"For you. For us. For the *gut* of our community."

He was offering her everything, just as Ethan had done. But this was so much different, because she loved Noah. "But we haven't even been courting."

He smiled. "Not in the conventional way."

She thought about him letting her use his *dawdy haus*, him taking out all the furniture she couldn't use, the desk he'd brought out for her, the exam table and bookshelf he'd built her—built *for* her—the filing cabinet he'd also built *for* her to put her records in—not that she had many yet—and putting in a telephone line, and standing up for her to even be able to start the clinic. And mostly preventing her from administering medical help in the beginning to show she could follow the leaders' instructions. "Sneaky. *Ja*, I'll marry you."

He took her in his arms and kissed her.

He pulled back. "I shouldn't have done that. We aren't married yet."

Kathleen shook her head. "I see nothing wrong in an engaged couple holding hands or sharing an occasional hug or kiss." She guessed that was her English side coming out.

"Your English side?"

"Do you mind?"

"Not in the least."

He glanced around and, after making sure they were alone, kissed her again. "We better go tell your parents. And the bishop."

Enveloped in his scent of wood and honey, Kathleen closed her eyes. "Once more."

She rose up on her tiptoes and kissed him again.

* * * * *

*If you loved this story,
be sure pick up these other
amazing Amish titles:*

*AN AMISH ARRANGEMENT
by Jo Ann Brown
A MAN FOR HONOR
by Emma Miller
AN UNEXPECTED AMISH ROMANCE
by Patricia Davids*

*Available now from Love Inspired!
Find more great reads at
www.LoveInspired.com*

Dear Reader,

Ahhhh, romance! I love romance. If there is a specific gene connected to romance, I must have it.

I hope you enjoyed the first of the Prodigal Daughters. Before starting to write an Amish romance, I had to get to know them a little. Like a lot of people, I had preconceived notions of who the Amish were. The more I researched, the more I fell in love with the Amish. I learned things I never imagined and discovered a vibrant people.

I had so much fun coming up with Amish women who didn't follow the traditional path for an Amish woman. So I thought, *What's something Amish almost never do?* Go to school beyond eighth grade. *So what would propel an Amish girl to defy her culture, religion and way of life.* I discovered it was *because* of those things she went against the rules. She loved her people so much, she was willing to sacrifice and endure ridicule to serve them.

I loved getting to know Kathleen and Noah. Though Kathleen might not have thought of herself as strong, she was strong indeed. She gave up her dream of her own family to go against hundreds of years of tradition and rules to provide her fellow Amish with medical care. Kathleen's prodigality was for a noble cause and not a selfish act.

Kathleen is dear to my heart not only because I admire her strength, but because I named her after my wonderful oldest sister.

Until next time, happy reading!

Blessings,
Mary

Get 2 Free Books,
Plus 2 Free Gifts—
just for trying the Reader Service!

Get 2 Free Books,

Plus 2 Free Gifts —

just for trying the Reader Service!

HARLEQUIN

HEARTWARMING™

HOME on the RANCH

HRCBPA18

READERSERVICE.COM

Manage your account online!

- Review your order history
- Manage your payments
- Update your address

**We've designed the
Reader Service website
just for you.**

Enjoy all the features!

- Discover new series available to you, and read excerpts from any series.
- Respond to mailings and special monthly offers.
- Browse the Bonus Bucks catalog and online-only exculsives.
- Share your feedback.

Visit us at:
ReaderService.com

RS16R